A PETAL IN THE WIND

A PETAL IN THE WIND is the first in a series of novels tracing the path of a young girl orphaned after a pogrom, following her life from Russia to Bohemia, through the grandeur of the art world, the hardship of World War I, the joy of love and marriage, and the tyranny under Nazi occupation.

A PETAL IN THE WIND

Miko Johnston

 Champlain Avenue Books, Inc.
Henderson, Nevada, USA

Published by Champlain Avenue Books, Inc., Henderson, Nevada

ISBN-13: 978-0-9896347-9-3
Library of Congress Control Number: 2014948326

Cover by LAWRENCE

FIRST EDITION
2014

Printed in the United States of America

Dedication

To Toiba (Tillie) Pearl, and especially to Edith—
See Mom, I listened

Acknowledgements

In the years since I began writing this novel, many eyes and voices helped me along the way, beginning with the Novel SIG of the *Alameda Writers Group*. Several members were there with me throughout most of the first draft, including Heather Ames, Bonnie Schroeder, Uriah Carr, Gayle Bartos-Pool, and Jackie Houchin. Their insight and encouragement helped me finish the manuscript. Later, fellow *Writers In Residence* members Rosemary Lord, Jackie Vick, Madeline Gornell, and Kate Thornton generously contributed their advice, as did Terry Carr, co-member of the *Pacific Online Writers Group*.

Special thanks to Becky Levine, who edited my first draft and helped guide me onto the next, hopefully improved version.

My gratitude to my four beta readers – Penny Lindenbaum, who kept me humble; Daune Hanson, who encouraged me to continue; Rowena Williamson, who cheered me on; and my husband Allan, who clarified my antecedents, expurgated my excessive "justs," and provided more encouragement than he'll ever know.

A Russian Shtetl in the Pale of Settlement
May, 1899

Chapter One

"Let me do it." Luska bounced in her chair as she repeated her plea to Mama. "I want to do it. Please say yes, Mama. Please," she begged, hands clenched to her chest.

Mama's eyes glowed with worry. "It's a big responsibility."

"I can do it. I'm almost eight."

"Will you lose your temper if someone bothers you?"

"No, Mama, I'll close my ears and keep walking."

"What if there's...trouble?" Mama always struggled to find the right word, but Luska knew she meant Cossacks, the violent marauders who attacked and plundered shtetls—the villages along the Western border where Jewish people were permitted to live.

"I'll run and hide underneath the nearest house, behind the stoop, like you taught me."

Mama rubbed her bulging tummy as her bright eyes turned quiet. "Go ahead, then." She lifted the earthenware jug from the shelf next to the stove and handed it to Luska.

Luska offered it back. "I can fetch more water if I take the pail."

"No. It would be too heavy for you to carry. This will do for now."

"Hooray, I'm fetching water." With the empty jug tucked under her arm, Luska rushed from the house to meet the timid sun, which still hid behind the walls of her shtetl. Every morning it clung to the land and peeked out before making its climb into the sky. She wondered if it, too, checked for Cossacks before coming out. Papa said they were safer here, far away from the bigger shtetls where most of the trouble happened. But a few months ago, Cossacks attacked

1

Papa in another village. Now she worried about them almost as much as Mama and Papa did.

Luska threaded her way through the narrow back streets to the well for the first time by herself. All the wooden houses along the street had finally shed their winter coat of snow; they showed off their stilted legs and high stoops like little girls in summer dresses.

Ahead, a family carried baskets toward the woods to forage for whatever spring bounty could be found, maybe the yellow mushrooms that Papa liked, or some early berries. After their day of rest, the villagers prepared for a new week every Sunday as if stirred from a great slumber. Everyone worked hard, for as the women would say, if you have nothing to do, it means you have nothing. Luska raised her jug to show the family that even though she was young, she, too, had an important chore to do, and was puzzled when the mother shook her head and turned away. Did the woman think she was bragging?

Luska waved to a peddler loading up his cart with tools, pots and pans. He must have spent all winter polishing his wares to look as good as new, like Papa used to do. Across the street, a horse with protruding ribs flicked its tail at flies while scrawny chickens circled its legs and pecked through weeds and wild grass. The yard had pole bean and pea vines curling up their stakes. Shoots of potatoes, onions, and beets sprang up in neat rows from everyone's garden now. Just weeks ago they were patch quilts of freshly hoed dirt.

"Hurry up or stand aside. I've two pails to fill." Mrs. Radovich's boy Lev waited behind her, arms crossed and foot tapping.

Luska stood on a broken crate at the well, ready to pump water, and she was not going to let this moment be ruined by the crowing of that freckle-faced teenager. She stretched until her fingertips locked around the pump handle and pulled as hard as she could. She could only bring it halfway down, and so it took extra pumps to fill her jug.

"How's a skinny little girl like you going to carry all that water? You'll drop it for sure," he chided.

"No I won't," she snapped, and almost said something mean to him, but she'd promised to be nice. "And I may be skinny now, but when I grow up I'll be tall and slender like my Mama," she added, but Lev had wandered off. What did he know? Papa always said elegant women were built like Mama, not plough horses.

Luska shook the water splashes from her hand and tried to lift the filled jug. "Oh, no," she moaned as it barely budged. "It's too heavy." She sipped some water off the top and tried again, finally picking up the jug and resting it against her body. The boy's teasing rang in her ears, and she wished she were a little bigger now.

Lev had gone off to flirt with Bella Vichenko, the farrier's daughter. Luska walked past them with a carefree smile that hid her efforts and took the surprise on his face as a compliment.

But soon the jug's weight made her arms tremble and shifting it didn't help. Every slosh of water slowed her pace and quickened her heart. If she spilled too much, or worse, dropped it, Mama and Papa wouldn't allow her to do this chore again until she was older. She chose a shorter route back, past small farms and peddler's homes that grew smaller and shabbier until she reached the shtetl's poor area, where people needed charity to survive.

The trembling worsened as she passed a row of tumbledown shacks pushed together like rotting teeth. The sun rose above their straw rooftops and warmed her face until sweat dribbled down her nose. She shook it off as a baby's cries broke the quiet Sunday morning.

3

Shouting erupted from the corner shack. She watched a little girl slink outside and dangle a bare leg off the top step. Luska smiled at her, but the poor girl stared back before lowering her head. The child's grim face saddened Luska, but something else, beyond the poverty, bothered her about the girl. She clutched her jug tighter and walked on. A thread of water seeped out the side and trickled down her hand. Mama had tried to seal the crack with candle wax, but it ran too deep.

When Luska finally reached home, she lumbered up the steps and, with a grunt she hoped Mama didn't hear, set their jug on the plankwood table.

"Did you have any problems?" Mama reached over to light the stove. Her dress no longer closed over her rounded belly and her nightgown showed between two straining buttons.

"The Radovich boy said I was too skinny to fetch water, but I told him I'd grow up to be just like you, not a plump chicken like his mama."

Mama looked horrified. "Luska, you didn't say that to him, did you?"

"Oh, no, you told me not to. I just thought it."

"Good," Mama said as she rubbed her belly. "If anyone's a plump chicken, it's me."

"Papa says you're not plump, you're stuffed."

"Did he?" Mama chuckled.

It was nice to see her happy, Luska thought.

With hands on hips, Mama arched her back and yawned, sending her black hair tumbling out of her colorful kerchief. Luska frowned. Why couldn't she have beautiful hair like Mama, not straight and the color of cooked meat? Everyone said "you have big brown eyes just like your Papa," but she had Mama's small nose and bow mouth, which was good. No girl should have a pear nose like Papa's.

"You're so lucky to have wavy hair," Luska observed.

Mama tucked Luska's chin-length hair behind her ears.

"When I was your age, my hair was straight, too, and I remember asking my mama if I'd ever have nice hair like hers. And when I grew up, she reminded me of that and we laughed about it. So I say your hair will be wavy like mine when you grow up and we'll laugh about it, too."

"And will I be as pretty as you, Mama?"

She swept Luska in her arms for a cuddle. "You already are, Luska, and every day I watch you grow more beautiful."

Luska breathed in the scent of musk as she nestled into Mama's warm body, her cheek against Mama's belly. She felt the baby inside move. With a giggle, she touched her fingers to the spot as Mama cuddled and rocked her, swaying to and fro. She could hear a heartbeat, but couldn't tell whose it was.

Mama kissed the top of Luska's head as she reached for the jug. "Oy, this is heavy. How did you manage it?"

She stood up straight. "I'm not a little girl anymore."

Mama filled the kettle and set it on the stove. "You are still a child, Luska." She measured tea into three glasses on the table.

"But I knew I could do it, and I wanted to do it, and…." The little girl flashed in her mind, the shouting in her house, the blank stare she gave Luska. Mama would say her eyes were empty. So were her hands. Empty, and still.

Idleness—that's what had bothered her. The village women were right. The poor had nothing to do, and they had nothing. By the time the kettle was boiling, Luska knew what to say.

"I did it because there's so much to do, and Papa can't do it, and it's too hard for you with your belly…and once the baby comes…. So you need me to do it."

"Is that why? I'm glad, then."

Luska thought that was a good answer until she looked at Mama. Her face smiled, but her eyes didn't.

5

"What else can I do?" Luska sipped her tea as Mama cut the heel of stale bread into three slices.

"I'll talk to Papa. He should be back now." She handed Luska a slice.

Luska dunked her bread in the hot liquid to soften it. After licking the crumbs from her hand, she followed Mama to the front yard to bring Papa his breakfast. He sat on one of three large rocks, set in crescent formation, where he carved his cart latches all day. Mama moved his crutch aside and put the hot glass on the rock next to the stump where his leg used to be.

"Did you let her go?" Papa asked.

Mama nodded.

"I wish she didn't have to." He gulped down his tea.

She took the empty glass and handed him his bread. "I wish she didn't want to."

He slipped an arm around the back of Mama's waist. She ran her fingers through his curly brown hair as he planted a kiss on her belly.

"You're bigger this time. Must be a boy." He gave her a little squeeze. A button on her dress popped off and landed almost a meter away. Luska ran to fetch it while Papa threw his head back and laughed and laughed until tears flowed from his eyes.

Luska laughed, too, but Mama didn't.

Papa laid down his knife. "Your Mama lost her sense of humor when I lost my leg."

Luska bit her lip. He lost his sense of humor, too, for his face looked troubled.

Mama took the button from Luska and put it in her pocket. "Let's pray this baby comes soon. We'll never have enough food to get through winter if I can't work the garden."

"You said the same thing when you were carrying Luska and we managed. Don't worry so much." He winked at

Luska. "Right, Lala?"

"Yes, Papa." Lala was his special name for her.

He beckoned Luska over and rested his palm on top of her head. "Look how much you've grown. Do you know how big you were last year?"

"No, Papa, how big?"

He lowered his hand until it reached her knees, as she knew he would.

"I wasn't that little," she giggled.

"No, but you were little enough to believe it then." He kissed her head, then went back to work.

She watched him stroke his knife over a stick until it became a peg. Wood shavings rained down with each swipe of the blade, like sparks from a fire. It was sad that Papa lost his leg and Mama always worried about money, but Luska liked that he stayed home all the time now.

"Did you sell another cart latch this morning?" Mama asked.

"Two, both to peddlers referred by Chelmsky. I should pay him a commission for all the business he's sent my way."

Mama plucked wood chips from his shirt.

"Mama, you always fuss over Papa when you have something to say but you don't want to say it."

"Luska!" Mama blustered.

But Papa laughed and he looked happy again. "She's getting as good as you at reading people. So what is it you don't want to tell me?"

Mama shook the chips from her hand. "Starting tomorrow I'm doing Chelmsky's laundry in exchange for credit in his butcher shop."

"Along with ours?" Papa's voice grew loud. "That's too much for you."

"Contrary to what you think, I am capable of working. Besides, how else will we be able to afford meat when the baby comes?"

7

"Mr. Chelmsky's a cousin," Luska reminded her. "He'd give us meat if we asked him."

Mama crossed her arms. "Take something without working for it? No Luska, that would be charity, and we don't take charity."

Luska flushed. "Is it a bad thing?"

"No, but it's not our way."

"Then can I do the laundry?"

"You're too young for that much responsibility."

"But I want to help. I can do it. You said I'm big enough to fetch water."

Papa raised his hand. "This is different, Luska. I don't want you leaving the shtetl."

If Papa called her Luska, it meant he was serious.

"Luska, I have another chore for you," Mama called to her from the garden.

Luska helped Mama to the ground to thin seedlings while she pulled weeds and Papa whittled. The sound of horses drew her attention to the street, where a baker's wagon parked near her house. The young driver had a nose bigger than Papa's.

"Good morning, Madam," he called out to Mama. "Would you like some bread today?"

She shook her head. "I think we have enough, thank you."

They had eaten the last of the bread for breakfast, but Mama's polite look meant "say nothing."

The man carried a dark loaf over to her. "This one is left from Friday. I could sell it to you for…half price?"

She waited until Papa lowered his head and nodded. He took the drawstring purse from his pocket and gave two coins to the bread man, who then handed Mama the loaf.

"You have a deal! Right, Papa?" Luska asked, but Papa stared at the ground.

Mama thanked the man with a weak smile. "Let's put this away," she told Luska.

After they entered the kitchen, Luska asked Mama, "Was Papa sad because he didn't make a good deal, or because he can't be a peddler anymore since he lost his leg?"

Mama wrapped the bread in paper. "I don't think it was either."

"Then what?"

"Luska, there are some things you're too young to understand." She checked the jug. "There's not enough water left for supper. Do you want to fetch it, or shall I?"

Luska bit her lip. She doubted she could carry another full jug, but she couldn't disappoint Mama. "How much will you need?"

Mama poured the rest of the water into a pot. "Half a jug will be enough."

Luska smiled. "I can do it."

"So can I, Luska."

"But Mama, I want to do it," Luska pleaded.

"Because you think I need you to do it."

"No, Mama, that's not why."

"Then tell me, because I can't understand it. All the other children would rather play than work, yet you always beg to fetch water, or weed, or do the laundry. Why do you want to do chores so much?"

"Because I love you."

Mama's mouth curled into a puzzled grin as she wrapped her arms around her daughter. "Then I must let you do chores, because I love you, too." She gave Luska a kiss before handing her the jug.

*   *   *   *   *

9

Two good pulls filled her jug halfway. It felt light enough to carry home with ease.

Bella Vichenko approached, wearing her best Sabbath dress, and on Sunday, the silly girl.

"Aren't you the latch maker's daughter?" Bella asked, tossing her head to show off the red ribbon she'd tied around her braid. She'd been talking to another boy right in front of Lev Radovich, who sat on a crate beside them with a sorrowful look on his face.

Luska nodded to Bella.

"Will those things really protect you from Cossacks," Bella asked.

"My Papa wouldn't be alive today if it wasn't for his latch."

"Maybe you should get one," Bella told the other boy in such a sweet voice it made Lev pout and hang his head.

Luska thought the girl was being mean. She pointed to Lev. "You should be nicer to him," she told Bella. "His family owns a cow."

The girl's eyes grew. She deserted the boy and sat next to a surprised Lev.

Luska left with her jug. As she neared her home, she heard someone call, "Wait!"

She turned around to find Lev running toward her with a bag.

"You were nice to me even though I teased you this morning. I want you to have this." He gave her the bag. "There's enough sugar and butter in here to make a cake. I was going to give it to Bella, but now I don't have to, after what you said."

Luska gulped. Butter and sugar were as good as coins. She thanked him and rushed home.

* * * * *

"My, what have you there?" Mama stared as Luska emptied the bag on the kitchen table. "Papa, our daughter's brought home the makings of a feast!"

Luska set the table while Mama prepared the cake. While it heated on the stove they ate beet soup with lots of onions, the way Mama liked it best, but Papa didn't complain about it.

"Luska, help me clear the table so we can enjoy our dessert," Mama said.

Luska was gathering up the bowls when Mama winced.

"Ow! Something bit me," she cried, slapping her leg. A spider fell and scurried away.

Startled, Luska let one bowl slip from her hand and it broke on the table, splashing beet soup on Mama's bodice. Mama rubbed it with a soapy rag, but the splotches didn't come out.

"It's stained," she moaned. "And my other dress is smaller than this one."

"I'm sorry. I didn't mean to break the bowl and ruin your dress."

Mama hugged Luska. "Don't cry. Nothing we have is more important than you."

After dinner, Luska helped Mama wash up.

Papa sat at the table. "Lala, let's practice our words. How do you say 'Good morning' in Russian?"

She knew that one. "Das vidanya."

"And in French?"

"Bonjour."

"What about…German?"

She wiped the bowl she was drying over and over to stall while she thought. "Um, Guten Tag."

They practiced other words for a while and she said most of them right.

"Very good. Now let's try some counting." Papa spread the money from his purse across the table as she sat beside him. "How many coins are there?"

She counted them quickly. "Eleven. Three big ones and eight small ones."

"That's right, how smart you are." He turned to Mama. "Do we owe anybody?"

"Not this week."

Papa held up a big coin. "If we don't need anything, we could give this to Chelmsky for credit. Then you wouldn't have to do his laundry."

"But Luska will outgrow her clothes by winter, and we don't have enough for the baby. I should buy some cloth."

"It's your decision, Mama."

"I say fabric; it lasts longer."

Mama sat in the kitchen, as she did most nights, humming to herself as she mended clothes. Papa sat beside her. She touched her belly and gazed at him, her face soft, her eyes bright with love.

Papa looked at Luska and said, "Do you know why I married your Mama?"

"No, Papa, tell me."

"Because she was the most beautiful girl in Moscow."

Mama smiled and her face lit up like the sun.

The house cooled quickly after sunset. Luska unrolled her bed and changed into her nightshirt. Mama started to tie the strings at the neckline.

"Let me do it, I can do it," Luska reminded her.

"I know you can, but I want to tonight." She fastened them into a bow.

"Sweet dreams." Mama kissed her forehead and tucked the thin blanket around her.

"Goodnight, Mama. Goodnight Papa." She nestled into bed, her head filled with plans for tomorrow, chores that needed to be done, ways she could help Mama and Papa…happy that she could…

Within moments she drifted off to sleep.

Chapter Two

Luska awoke to find Mama still lying on her mattress, her leg twitching under the threadbare quilt, her face knotted with worry.

"What's wrong, Mama? Is the baby coming?"

"No, but get Papa."

Luska raced to the door and called to him before returning to Mama's side.

Papa came quickly. He moved Luska away from the bed and pulled back the covers to reveal Mama's leg, all red and swollen below the knee.

"I can make a compound to draw out the venom, but you must stay off your feet."

"I can't, there's too much to do...the garden, the laundry," she protested.

Luska couldn't tell if the pain in Mama's face was because her leg hurt, or that she couldn't do her chores. She piped up, "Let me do the laundry, Papa."

"No, Luska, I've already told you this is not a chore for a child."

"But I'm not a little girl anymore," she insisted. "I want to help. I can do more things for you and Mama, if you'll let me."

"I know, and I appreciate all you've done, but don't be in such a hurry to grow up."

Mama squirmed on the mattress until she managed to sit up. "I think we should let her, Papa. We're so far behind, and I promised Chelmsky."

"You expect too much from her."

Mama's mouth quivered. She looked ready to cry.

"At least your burden is temporary," Papa muttered, his voice cracking. "Whenever I drove my cart past a fine home, I'd think how someday a girl as spirited as my little Lala would catch the eye of a rich merchant's son." He slapped his stump. "But what can I offer her now?"

"Since when have you shown any talent for predicting the future?" Mama said.

"It's not right."

"I don't like it, either. But Papa, we have to let her go."

Papa's shoulders dropped and he curled himself so tightly around his crutch he almost shrank before Luska's eyes. He hobbled to the kitchen. "Do we have enough water left for tea?"

Papa made breakfast before returning to his carving.

Mama fidgeted in her bed as she watched Luska gather the laundry and roll it into a tight ball. "Will you remember what I told you to do?"

"Yes, Mama."

"And don't forget to—"

"To pick up Mr. Chelmsky's laundry. I remembered."

"I should have known. Let me see what you have."

Luska brought over the ball of laundry.

"Are you sure you have everything there? It looks too small."

"I pressed my knees into the bundle so I could wrap it tight, like you told me. And see how I made a strap out of Papa's shirt sleeve."

Mama cupped Luska's face in her hand. "Ah, how could such a big girl fit inside such a small child? Go, and try to get that stain out of my dress…scrub everything well."

Luska went to the door. "I will Mama. I'll do a very good job. You'll see." She draped the laundry over her shoulder and climbed down the steps. The sun warmed her bare legs.

Papa beckoned to her from his carving rock. "Lala, come here, I have a present for you."

As she approached, he wrapped his arm around her and gave her a noisy kiss on her cheek. She giggled as she kissed him back. Papa gave the best presents.

He cupped his ear. "Do you hear that?"

Luska tried by copying him. "No, Papa, what is it?"

"It's God's music. You can hear it in the breezes rustling the leaves and the chatter of birds, waters rushing through the river and raindrops striking the roof. When the winds howl through the trees or thunder roars from the heavens, it's there, too. Listen for it once more."

She cupped her ear again. Sounds drifted in from the nearby meadow.

"I can hear it now."

"Good. Take it with you."

Luska wound through back streets until she reached the main road, a stretch of big houses with shops in front and tradesmen's homes in back. Up ahead, three women in patched dresses hurried toward the outskirts of town with their piles of laundry. A stout red-faced woman bounded out of a house with a sagging porch. Sofia, the midwife, balanced two huge loads of wash on her shoulders.

"Good morning, Luska. Your mother's due soon, no?"

"Papa says she's going to have a boy this time."

Sofia laughed. "Men always say that. We'll know soon enough," She grunted as she rolled her shoulders forward, shifting her load. "Mondays are very busy at the river. I have to hurry, or the best spots will be taken. Good luck, child."

She marched ahead to join the other women as Luska approached Mr. Chelmsky's butcher shop, where two strapping horses were hitched outside. She entered through the weatherworn door to find a young man with a pebbly face and an older bald man inside. The strangers leaned against the counter, watching Mr. Chelmsky perform a dramatic story she'd heard many times.

"...then Cossacks raid the shtetl! They attack him, but he has a surprise. The peddler throws the latch, detaches his horse from the wagon, and rides off. But his trick enrages the Cossack bandits. They give chase as their horses tear through the burning village. Just as he reaches the outskirts, they encircle him, roaring and cursing as they draw their sabers to attack!"

His raised arm whipped around as though he were fighting Cossacks, too.

"Did he escape unharmed?" interrupted the young man.

"They land one blow which slices deep into the peddler's thigh. The wound becomes infected, and by the time he arrives home, the leg has to be taken. But each dawn brings a promise new. Our Rabbi, being a wise man, tells everyone how this escape latch saved the peddler's life. Soon, men like you are traveling to our village to buy them for their wagons."

He patted his round belly as he gestured toward Luska.

"In fact, this girl's father owes his life to the latch, doesn't he?"

"Yes, that's true."

Mr. Chelmsky winked at her and she managed not to giggle.

"So is this what you gentlemen came searching for?"

The bald man's face smiled but his eyes didn't. "I think we've found the right village."

The young man looked very grave. "We'll return soon...to place our order."

Luska waited until the men walked out.

"That was wonderful, Mr. Chelmsky. You tell that story so well. Papa will make a lot of money now, thanks to you."

"Let's hope I persuaded them. So, what brings you in, little one?"

She propped her bundle against the counter. "Mama said I could do the laundry."

His eyes widened and his hands flew to his head.

"Laundry? Today? Oh my, I completely forgot. What am I going to do?"

Luska knew he was teasing, for she had already spotted his load of wash behind a crate. Giggling, she scooted over to the pile and held up an apron stained with meat blood.

"Ha, you caught me!" He reached under his counter for a wad of paper.

"When you come back, remind me to give you some of this cheese to take home. Mrs. Radovich paid her bill with it, but there's too much for one person."

"You don't have to give us anything. You've done so much for us already."

He opened the package and broke off a chunk. "I tell you what. Take this piece with you and have it as a treat. If you don't like it, then don't take the rest. But if you do...." He gave her the piece and stowed the rest behind his counter.

"As Papa always says, 'You have a deal.'" She began rolling Mr. Chelmsky's laundry into a ball. "Who were those men?"

"Farmers from another village. They met a peddler who had one of your Papa's latches, and now they want to buy some."

She frowned. "I didn't like them. They were ugly."

"Not every man can be as handsome as me." He ran his hand over his thick silver hair.

"I'm glad you didn't tell them I was the peddler's daughter. Strangers make me worry about..." her voice dropped to a whisper, "Cossacks."

Chelmsky clucked and waggled his finger. "Don't pay attention to those stories. The village women love to gossip and the men like to dramatize, like I just did, to make it sound more exciting. But we haven't seen a Cossack, let alone an attack, this far from Moscow in years, so stop worrying. After all, why would they come out here when there are plenty of shtetls to pillage back east."

"I ought to go or there'll be no place left for me at the river." She hung his wash load over her shoulder. "And don't you worry. I'll do a good job and get your laundry all clean."

"I know you will, Luska, you're a clever girl. I'll see you later."

She caught the two strangers huddled in conversation when she left the shop. They stopped talking when they saw her. Just looking at them made her skin prickle.

The men smiled at her, and she thought about what Mr. Chelmsky had said.

"We've never seen a Cossack, let alone an attack, this far from Moscow…."

She smiled back and headed for the river. As she neared the entrance gate to the village the men galloped past her at breakneck speed. The hairs stood up on the back of her neck. She could have sworn she heard them laughing.

When Luska arrived at the river bend, where it widened before splitting into two branches, the other women had taken up every spot along the bank. They stopped washing and gossiping long enough to show her the path that followed the smaller stream. Her regret at being chased off soon turned to pleasure as she walked through the woods. The tree branches and leaves painted pictures of golden light and deep shadow across the floor of the forest. She enjoyed God's

20

music along the way – the swish of branches, water splashing, birds singing – and before midday she came upon a small clearing, where the stream ended in a pond ringed by tall trees.

By the time the sun had dipped below the midpoint in the sky, most of the wash lay drying across the rocks. Luska finished her cheese before checking the bodice of Mama's dress. She hadn't been able to wash the stains out. A sense of laziness pricked at her until she tried again, scrubbing even harder, but the red splotches wouldn't go away, nor did the memory of her clumsiness last night.

She rehung the dress over a low branch and gathered the rest of the wash, starting with the linens. I'll put everything into one bundle and separate it at Mr. Chelmsky's shop, she thought as she folded towels. Then he'll have time to wrap up some cheese for me to take home. Mama and Papa will say, "How clever of you," and then maybe Mama won't be too upset that I ruined her dress.

She lifted her family's Sabbath tablecloth from a branch with care. The precious heirloom had been handed down from mother to daughter, and each woman added something to the design. Mama had embroidered a pair of candlesticks, using real gold thread for the candle's flames. Luska held it under a sunbeam to make it gleam like fire. The candlesticks flanked the loaf of challah stitched by her grandmother. When her time came, Luska would add something special, too; the yellow Bohemian crystal goblet. Her fingertip traced its shape on a bare corner of the cloth as she remembered the day Papa brought it home two winters ago.

"How will I tell Mama about this?" Papa wondered aloud.

Luska curled up in Papa's lap. After listening to him repeat the story many times, it didn't sound as scary. She touched the goblet.

"Can I hold it, Papa?"

21

"Alright, but be careful. If it falls it will break." He handed it to her.

It felt heavy for its size. Her little fingers wrapped around the clear stem and base. The yellow bowl sparkled in the lamplight, like sunshine in summer.

"It's pretty, Papa."

He kissed the top of her head. "You should have pretty things, my little Lala, more than your poor Papa can give you. But someday you will…."

She swirled her fingers in the pond and watched the ripples shimmer outward until the surface stilled into a mirror. Draping the tablecloth over her shoulders, she stood and promenaded along the water's edge, glimpsing at her reflection. "Look at me, dressed like a queen, like Esther in the Bible. She must have worn dresses sewn with gold thread, too."

Luska turned and announced to the trees, "I am Queen Lala, and this is my land. In the shtetl, everyone worries. Will there be sickness, or bad weather that ruins the crops? But in my land, you'll grow plenty of food in summer, and have stoves to heat the forest in winter. All I ask is that you show me how you grow new leaves and branches, so I can help Papa grow a new leg. How do you answer?"

Cheers and applause erupted from the clearing, then faded into the sound of rustling leaves. A chill ran through her. The damp cloth had soaked through to her skin. She folded the tablecloth and straightened her gray dress, the one Mama fashioned out of Papa's old shirt. Queen Lala indeed, Luska thought as she gathered the dried clothing.

She took care folding the rest of the laundry, for although there was still much to do at home, she liked being here and did not want to hurry. Then a shrill noise, coming from the direction of her village, grew closer and louder. She looked skyward as dozens of screeching birds soared above the pond and suddenly vanished over the treetops. A bad feeling settled upon her like the shadow from a storm cloud. She quickened her pace until everything had been rolled into her bundle, but it didn't ease her sense of dread.

Another garment floated near the mouth of the pond. She plucked Mr. Chelmsky's shirt out, rung it dry, and held it up to the sun. Something had turned it pink. She decided to ask the other women down river how that could have happened.

Luska tied the shirt around her waist and began the long walk home.

Chapter Three

A tailwind snapped against Luska's back like a scolding hand prodding her along the deserted path. It wasn't a chill that penetrated her bones and left her shivering. Ever since she'd heard the birds screaming, something had felt wrong and it grew with every step, every glance. Shafts of light shot through the trees and crashed against the ground. Branches flailed, leaves hissed, water gurgled and gasped across the rocks in the stream. The forest sounded off-key to her, made worse by a peculiar silence from the birds. What had happened to God's music?

As she neared the river, the wind vanished and an odd smell invaded the woods, like when Mama singed the pinfeathers from a chicken, only worse. Much worse. It turned her stomach. Rattled, she ran to the clearing to join the women.

She slid through the dense brush and froze. Bodies. Twenty, maybe more. Floating in bloody water. Tangled in shreds of cloth. Her bundle dropped, her hands slammed over her mouth, forcing the scream back into her throat.

More bodies blocked the spillway. Lapping water bumped another against them.

A dozen women lay slaughtered, twisted into inhuman positions, across the bloodstained riverbank. One, on her back, eyes and mouth agape, terror frozen on her face.

Sofia, the midwife.

The smell dragged Luska back. She saw columns of smoke rising over the treetops coming from the direction of the shtetl. Shock and fear wrestled in the pit of her stomach.

Cossacks!

She grabbed her bundle and raced home, her mind spinning with the violent tales she'd heard whispered in shops

25

and at family gatherings. Within minutes Luska reached the outskirts of the village. Dark plumes slithered toward the milky tea sky. She approached the gate with caution.

Gasping for breath, she entered the shtetl. Heat shimmied from the ashes and shattered the air above like broken glass. Everything ahead looked bent and folded, from the buckled ruins along the main road clear out to the meadow beyond.

No birds chattered, no horses whinnied, no chickens screeched, no men shouted for their wives, no women screamed for their children, no babies cried for their mothers. An ungodly stillness blanketed the village, save for the crackling of torched wood.

Stumbling through the destruction until the smell of death sickened her to the point of dizziness, she collapsed to her knees and retched herself dry. Still dazed, she steadied herself on a rock as she forced herself to stand. Nearby, two more large rocks sat in crescent formation. It took a moment to realize that the pile of blackened wood and smoldering rubble behind the boulders was all that was left of her home.

"Mama! Mama," she cried. "Where are you?"

Silence.

"Papa, can you hear me?" All she heard was the violent pounding of her heart. She tore through the remains, looking for a sign that Mama and Papa survived, that trapped somewhere underneath the rubble, they were still alive. Her hand gripped any solid piece she felt – a shard of pottery, a spoon, some nails. An ember burned her palm and she cried out in pain, but she kept searching through the debris until she felt something hard. As she pulled it out, yellow shone through the ash. The Bohemian crystal goblet survived, undamaged! She cradled it like a baby as she stowed her precious find inside her laundry bundle.

Papa. Mama.

"What if there's...trouble?"

"I'll run to the nearest house and hide underneath, behind the stoop, like you taught me."

She focused her search in the area where the stoop had been, but found nothing. Frantic, she lifted a few more boards and ran her hands underneath until her fingers locked onto something that felt long and slender. Encouraged, she lifted it out of the ashes. At first, she thought the charred piece could be a furniture leg, narrowed at one end, until she saw the crusted remains of fingers. She dropped it with a scream, snatched her bundle and ran.

Luska had no idea how long she had wandered through the destroyed village. She finally dropped to the ground near a collapsed building and hugged herself as she rocked on her knees, wondering what to do, where to go...this place couldn't be her home, not now. Visions of that crusted hand, all she could find of her parents, tormented her. She tried shaking the image from her head, but it was seared into her memory and no amount of head shaking would make it go away. She started to cry.

"What will I do," she wailed.

A muffled groan came from beneath the wreckage. She approached with caution. Wrapping the bloodstained shirt around her hand for protection, she peeled off layers of blackened wood until she saw the burned torso of a man. She jumped back. His ghastly appearance petrified her until she realized this was the first living soul she'd found in the shtetl. Trembling, she moved closer to remove the debris from his upper body.

"Who...who are you, sir?"

Another groan.

She uncovered his face, blistered and red, but recognized him immediately.

"Mr. Chelmsky!" Part of her wanted to bury her face in his neck and cry, but he was so badly disfigured she was too afraid to touch him.

27

He lay gasping for air. His eyes finally focused on Luska. The sight of her alive and unhurt seemed to comfort him. He struggled to speak, but no words came out. Luska moved her ear closer to his mouth. He finally managed to whisper a word, and then fell silent. She knelt beside him, upset and confused, hoping she had misheard, but his steady, calm gaze upon her left no doubt of what he'd said, no choice of what to do. His eyes closed as he took his final breath. She untied his shirt from around her waist and draped it over his face.

Tears streaming, she rose and clutched her bundle of laundry so tightly her fingers turned white. All he had said was, "Go". She ran toward the woods and the setting sun.

Chapter Four

Luska hurried through the canopy of trees to the stream, holding her breath as she passed the river filled with the dead. She heard no music, only silence, as though a veil of mourning had fallen over the land. Twilight approached and the thought of being alone in the woods after dark terrified her. Shrill cries pierced the sky and she jumped, sending her ball of laundry tumbling out of her hands. A hawk circled above the treetops, hunting for prey. As quiet fell upon the woods again, she picked up her bundle and hastened toward the small clearing where trees ringed the pond.

Before long the sun disappeared, but Luska remembered the path well enough to retrace her steps. An oval moon shed its cold light through the trees and across the floor of the woods.

As she approached the pond, loud voices and horses snorting disrupted the silence. Cossacks! Her heart pounded so loudly it almost drowned out the sounds coming from their camp. She backed up until she couldn't hear them anymore, then sat under a tree and cried, wishing she could be home with her family. She shut her eyes tight.

Papa smiled and beckoned Luska over. He rested his hand on top of her head.

"Look how much you've grown, Lala. Do you know how big you were last year?"

"No, Papa, how big?"

He lowered his hand until it reached her knees, as she knew he would.

"I wasn't that little," she giggled.

"No, but you were little enough to believe it a year ago." He kissed her head.

Eerie sounds crept through the night, dragging her back to the forest. She pressed against the tree, her eyes darting in every direction, too frightened to move but more frightened to stay. Ghastly images flickered in her mind, of bodies floating in the river, of smoke rising from the ashes of the shtetl, of poor Mr. Chelmsky.

Mr. Chelmsky. "Go," he had told her, but where? She shook her head to clear away the bad visions and wondered if she would make it through the night.

"I know you will, Luska. You're a clever girl."

She swallowed hard, trying to force down her fears like bitter medicine.

"Mama, Papa, what should I do?"

A beam of light fell across her legs. She looked up and saw the half-moon hiding behind the leaves. A little bigger than last night. It was growing.

Mama cupped Luska's face in her hand. "Ah, how could such a big girl fit inside such a small child?"

I'll follow the path of the moon tonight, she thought, and tomorrow I'll follow the sun.

She walked through the unfamiliar landscape, humming softly to drown out the sounds haunting the darkness. She wrapped Papa's shirt around her as much for comfort as for warmth. The moon began its descent and the woods quieted until all she could hear was the crunch of leaves beneath her feet.

The sound of rushing water urged her ahead. She stumbled upon a stream hidden behind some brush. After bringing handful after handful of water to her lips, she laid her head on her bundle and surrendered to exhaustion.

Snow had been falling for three days and the barn felt cold. She watched as Papa tried to add another pot to the frame of his cart.

"There's no more room, Papa. Why are you taking so much this time?"

Papa hung the pot over a smaller one. He beckoned her to

come closer. "As soon as the roads are passable, I'm leaving for a while."

"How long will you be away?"

"A long time. At least three full moons and three new moons."

"Why are you going away for so long?"

"I want to combine two trips into one, so I can make enough money to stay home when Mama has the baby." He stroked her hair.

"I still say it's too risky." Mama stood in the doorway. "You've spent all our savings for this trip. What if the villagers have no money? And what about the Cossacks? It's not safe where you're going." She hit a pot, and they all banged and clanged.

"Papa's not afraid of Cossacks, Mama."

"Then he's a fool," she snorted.

"Am I? Come see this." He motioned her over to the front of his cart.

In one hand, Papa held up a wood frame with a short peg that stuck up. In the other hand he had a second frame, wrapped in wire, which he locked firmly around the peg. He pulled on them to show how strong they were when connected. Then, with a quick upward snap of the latch, the two pieces instantly separated.

"What is that?" Mama's voice softened.

Papa beamed. "It's a safety latch I designed for the wagon. At the first sign of trouble, I jump on the horse and lift this piece to disconnect the cart. The Cossacks take the merchandise while I escape, poor but alive. How many peddlers are killed trying to save their wagons?"

"Too many." Mama was thinking about that. "Poor but alive."

"I can't feed my family if I'm dead."

Mama steadied the pot and the barn was quiet again.

"You're right. Better to live and start again."

*   *   *   *   *

31

Morning's first light glazed the surface of the stream.

Luska lay half awake, cradled in her sweet dream, until the chattering of birds forced her eyes open. She sat up and looked around. Reality set in and ripped away her blanket of joy with the last streaks of darkness, leaving her frightened, hungry, and longing for Mama and Papa. She sat a while, hugging her knees to her chest, as her head filled with questions about the uneasy day ahead. Would she find food, or water? Could there be a storm? What if she chanced upon bad people, like Cossacks? What if she encountered no one?

As the sun rose, thin clouds stretched across the sky until they disappeared. Time to face the unknown path that lay before her. She washed herself and drank her fill of water before setting out into the forest, following the direction of the shadows.

Chapter Five

Another night and day passed before Luska reached a small village near the edge of the forest, the first sign of people she'd stumbled upon along her journey, the first chance to put something in her belly besides water and find better shelter than a tree.

A patchwork of stone houses, chicken coops and gardens bordered the dusty streets, with laundry hanging on clotheslines and rows of vegetables sprouting in the yards. It looked so much like her shtetl she began to cry. She wanted to run into the village and shout, "I'm hungry. Please give me something to eat." But a voice rang in her ears.

Mama folded her arms. "Take something without working for it? No Luska, that would be charity, and we don't take charity."

Luska flushed. "Is it a bad thing?"

"No, but it's not our way."

She leaned against a tree and held her groaning belly. A sudden wind passed through the treetops, rustling the branches. Luska looked up.

Papa showed her the goblet.

"Papa, it's pretty. Where did you find this?"

"In a town where no one wanted to buy anything from me. Can you imagine that?"

She shook her head in disbelief.

"So I told the townspeople, if they can't afford to pay me for my wares, I'd consider taking something in trade. Then an ex-soldier of the Czar offered me this goblet and a tiny ball of gold thread in exchange for tools, pots and cloth."

"And you made the deal, Papa?"

"No, I made him a counter offer more favorable to me. The soldier considered it for a moment, then whipped his saber from its

sheath and held it at my throat!"

She gasped. "What did you do?"

"I agreed. Better to be poor but alive. You can't feed your family if you're dead."

The wind died and the sounds of the forest returned.

Mama and Papa wouldn't want her to take charity, but she could sell or trade some of her laundry for what she needed. As fearful as she was about approaching strangers, the thought of spending another night without food or shelter scared her even more. She took a deep breath and, with Papa's stories about his peddling days running through her mind, walked to the village.

She chose a house with a large vegetable garden to begin. Heavy footsteps rang out before the door opened to reveal a stocky woman carrying a broom in one hand and soiled rags in the other. Her dirt-stained apron covered a faded dress with more patches than stars in the night sky. She acknowledged Luska's presence with a scowl.

Luska stiffened at the sight of the woman's puffy face, squinting eyes and tufts of gray hair poking out of her kerchief.

"What do you want?" the woman demanded.

Luska began to tremble. She caught her breath and answered. "Good afternoon, Madam." She gave a slight curtsey. "I have clothing for sale or trade. Would you like something?"

The woman said nothing.

Luska presented two shirts, but her customer waved her away.

"They're all wrinkled."

"They were just washed, Madam."

"Why would I want things that need to be ironed?"

Luska stepped forward. "I'll iron them for you. Let me do it."

The woman raised her eyebrow. "You don't know how to use an iron, do you?"

Luska lowered her head. "No..." she mumbled before looking up to meet the woman's face. "But if you show me how, I'll iron everything in your house for a meal and a place to stay."

"Child, I don't have time to teach you. Go away!" She slammed the door in Luska's face.

Hunger gnawed at her empty belly. She left quickly, before the woman's vegetable garden tempted her to do something bad.

At the next house she faced a thin young man smoking a pipe.

"Good afternoon, sir. I have some fine clothing for—"

The door closed. She fought the urge to cry and went on.

Several more attempts were unsuccessful. One woman tried to grab her merchandise, but Luska tore it from her grasp and raced away down the street, past houses and farms, until exhaustion overtook her. She stumbled and fell breathless in the middle of the road.

The cackle of hens drew her attention to a woman feeding chickens in a yard across the way. Luska could hear the sounds of children's voices coming from inside her house.

The woman stood as tall as Mama, with the same round belly, long neck and slender arms poking through threadbare sleeves. She had a rag tied around her head, and wavy hair spilling halfway down her back, as thick and nearly as dark as Mama's, except for the patches of silver above her ears. She looked so much like....

"What are you staring at?" the woman snapped. The harsh tone felt like a slap.

Luska flinched. "I'm sorry, I...." She got to her feet and rubbed her skinned knees as she blinked back tears. With great difficulty she took a deep breath for courage and forced herself to look the stern woman in the eye.

"Good afternoon, Madam. I have some clothing for sale or trade." She fumbled with her merchandise. "Would you like something?" She held up Mr. Chelmsky's clothes.

"No. And stop staring at me, I don't like it!"

Luska misted up. "You have beautiful hair, just like my Mama."

The woman cocked her head and eyed Luska with suspicion. "I've never seen you before. Are you from the gypsy camp?"

"No, Madam."

"Then where did you come from?"

Luska pointed in the direction from which she'd traveled. "I walked from my village, about three days from here."

"Who brought you here, child?"

"No one, I came here by myself."

The woman snorted. "You expect me to believe that? Where is your family?"

Caught off guard by the question, Luska choked back a sob. "Dead, Madam. Killed by Cossacks a few days ago. They killed everyone in our village, then they burned it to the ground. Everything's gone." Tears washed down her cheeks and splashed onto the dry road. "There's nobody left but me."

The woman stiffened; her eyes bright with anger.

"Cossacks, bah!" She spat on the ground. "Worse than the gypsies. Spawns of the devil, they are, they should all rot in hell." She spat again and took a deep breath.

Luska felt a connection with this woman after her outburst. She loosened her bundle.

"Mama always wore a colorful kerchief. She said even if she had to wear rags, she would always have a nice headscarf to show off her hair. You should have something nice for your hair, too." She held up a red kerchief with yellow, green, and black embroidery. "You don't have to give

36

me money for it. I'll trade it for food."

The woman's arms circled her belly. She said nothing.

Luska took a step forward. "All I want is something to eat." She held the kerchief up higher so the woman could see the detailed needlework. "Please. I'm so hungry."

The woman's gaze shifted between Luska and the red kerchief she held out.

"Let me see that." Her voice softened a little.

Luska hesitated before depositing the kerchief in the woman's outstretched hand. Her customer held it up to the light, inspecting it for signs of wear.

"All I have is some bread. I'll give you a...two pieces for this."

The kerchief was worth more than that, but Luska needed food, and this woman had no interest in bargaining. She thought of Papa's deal with the soldier. Hunger cut as deeply as an unsheathed saber to the neck. Reluctantly, she nodded.

The woman went into her house and returned shortly with two thick slices of bread and a small chunk of cheese. Luska bounced with joy. The woman looked almost as happy.

"Oh, thank you, you are very kind and very generous, Madam."

"I'm Mrs. Kasyanov." She removed the old rag from her head and tucked it into her pocket. "No one in this village can afford to take in an orphan, but you can travel with my husband tomorrow."

"Where?"

"To the city, the largest in the region. Many people live there."

"Thank you, but how can I repay you?"

The woman fixed on Mr. Chelmsky's trousers. "My husband could use some new clothes. Come back this evening. I'll let you sleep in the wagon tonight."

Mrs. Kasyanov tied Mama's kerchief around her head.

"Be ready to leave at dawn. The trip there will take all day, and there may be danger on the road, but it's your best chance to find help."

Chapter Six

Luska cowered against the wall in a narrow alleyway, tucked back from the stone covered road, and covered her ears. Dozens of horse drawn wagons clattered back and forth past the tallest houses she'd ever seen. People rushed along crowded streets, their heels and canes hitting the pavement added to the din.

Patches of mold on the wall bothered her nose and the smell from a nearby garbage heap made her eyes water. Still, she couldn't bring herself to move from the spot where Mr. Kasyanov had left her some time ago, so overwhelmed were her senses by the bustle of the city. He had explained in which direction and how far she should walk to find the central square, but all she could manage so far was to watch the noisy activity all around her and wonder how this place could be so different from the forest, yet in some ways be the same – much bigger than she could have imagined and every bit as scary.

The snap of a horsewhip startled her. She ran from the safety of the alley as a uniformed man on horseback tore through the passageway and galloped down the road. The constant strike of hooves against stone echoed like thunder. People streamed past her as she stood alone in the street, her body casting a long shadow. Daylight would end soon, and with it, her best chance of finding food and shelter in this strange place. She clutched her bundle, now half its size after bartering with the Kasyanovs, and began to walk.

The houses grew larger as she neared the town square. She heard rustling above, and looked up in time to see a woman with a bucket lean out of a third story window. Luska flattened herself against the wall moments before a stream of dirty water hit the street and splashed up, splattering her dress with gray droplets. She straightened her skirt as best as she could before continuing on.

She passed a shop with many tables and chairs set up for dining. The scent of cooking escaped and danced around her like a temptress. She ran her tongue over her parched lips, hoping to catch some of the flavor, but all she licked off was dust.

Ahead lay the town square, a large open plaza filled with market stalls surrounded by shops and grim looking buildings of gray stone. Crowds of people milled through the square, examining the wares hung from stall frames and displayed in shop windows. Some chatted with merchants. Others haggled for the best price. Everyone seemed to be loud and in a great hurry.

Luska remained still for a moment and wondered what she should do now, when a flash of yellow next to a storefront attracted her. The noise dulled and the crowd melted into a blur as she walked toward the corner shop, where color-filled buckets lined up in front of a wide window beckoned her. As she approached, so did a tall, lean man dressed in fine clothes. The shop door suddenly swung open before her and a squat man with a big red moustache burst out of the shop, almost knocking her over.

"Mr. Prodan, good to see you," the shopkeeper said to the tall man as they shook hands.

She walked past them and returned her attention to a display of the most beautiful flowers she had ever seen. Each bucket overflowed with blossoms in every color imaginable, but the flowers at the far end of the row called to her until she stood a nose away from their cups of golden petals. They looked like the Bohemian crystal goblet that lay hidden inside her belongings. She tightened her grip on her bundle, knowing that if even one finger were free, she would touch a flower. Instead, all she dared to do was lean over and sniff it, to see if it smelled as pretty as it appeared.

"Lala."

Luska spun around, searching for the voice that called to her.

"Lala." It was Mr. Prodan, the tall man who had been greeted by the flower merchant. Her eyes fixed on him. How did he know her, and by her special name, the one only Papa used?

"Lala," he repeated. "That's what they're called. In some places they're known as tulips. They're a most unusual flower, very beautiful, aren't they?"

She lowered her head and nodded. "Oh. I thought you were calling me."

Mr. Prodan smiled. "Are you called Lala?"

She nodded again.

He walked over to the bucket filled with golden tulips, plucked one out, and presented it to her. She hesitated, unsure if she should accept it. He pressed the flower to his chest for a moment. Then his arm swept toward her in grand style; his hand turned over and he opened his fingers. The tulip lay unprotected across his palm, waiting for her to take it. This time, she did.

"A beautiful name for a beautiful child." He tipped his hat to her and walked away.

She froze for a moment, stunned by what had just happened, and watched as he rounded the corner before running after the man, barely able to keep pace with his broad stride. He continued down another busy street, with Luska right behind him, holding her flower in one hand and her bundle in the other.

He stopped near the next corner in front of what looked like a peddler's wagon, except it was bigger and finer than any she had seen before, laden with shiny tools and unfamiliar objects made of metal. The merchandise hanging from its frame seemed new. A fair-haired boy about thirteen stood by the wagon. Mr. Prodan tossed him a coin before the boy tipped his cap and dashed off.

He noticed Luska as he was about to mount his wagon.

"Why Lala, what are you doing here?" He patted her head and smiled at her.

She held up the flower.

"Did you think I stole that? The florist is a friend of mine. I will pay him when I return on Monday, so you needn't worry about either of us getting into trouble."

"It's the most beautiful thing I've ever seen, and you were very kind to give it to me, but I don't know why."

"Dear child, it's a gift. Keep it."

Mr. Prodan climbed up into his wagon and lifted the reins. Luska held fast to the side panel as tightly as she could, as though it would stop him from leaving.

"If you please, sir, tell me why? Are you sure you don't know me?"

Mr. Prodan let the reins slacken.

"What an odd question," he laughed. "Hasn't anyone ever done something nice for you?"

"Yesterday, a woman gave me cheese with my bread in trade for clothing because I was very hungry, and her husband let me ride with him to this place so I might find some food and a place to stay."

"You don't live in the city?"

Luska told him everything that happened as best as she could, from the time she left the pond with her laundry until he called to her in the town square. The most dreadful things were hard to say out loud, but whenever she paused, Mr. Prodan would nod and urge her to continue. He listened intently, stroking his beard the whole time. His face reddened when she mentioned the Cossacks.

"They're getting more brazen by the hour. Hardly a day goes by without hearing of an attack. We used to say, 'To succeed in business, move forward and don't look back,' but no longer. Even a traveling salesman isn't safe anymore. I lost one wagon to those bandits already."

"Then let me go with you. I'll help you. I know all about how to sell things, my Papa taught me. Please, Mr. Prodan, I can do it."

"I'm sorry, but you can't come with me, I have no way to take care of you. What you need is a family who will take you in. You're a sweet little girl, I'm sure someone will."

"But I don't know anybody in the city except you. Do you know of a family who might want me?"

He thought long and hard before shaking his head. "I feel badly that I can't do more to help you. It's almost dark, too. You can't be wandering the streets at night, it isn't safe. Why don't you spend the night behind the flower shop and continue your search for help in the morning."

It took great effort to hide her disappointment. "I'll go there right away. Thank you for my flower, Mr. Prodan, and for trying to help me. You've been very kind; may it keep you safe from Cossacks."

He gathered up the reins again. "Thank you, that's very kind. You know, Lala, I had a run in with those thugs a few months ago."

"When the Cossacks took your wagon. That happened to my Papa, too. I'm sure you were very brave like he was."

"More lucky than brave, I must confess. At least I managed to get away, thanks to a little secret I discovered."

A secret. She looked to the sky.

There was Papa in the barn. In one hand, he held up a wood frame with a short peg that stuck up. In the other hand he had a second frame with a metal piece that he locked firmly around the peg. He pulled on them to show how strong they were when connected. Then, with a quick upward snap of the metal latch, the two pieces instantly separated.

"Do you have one of Papa's latches?" She checked his cart for the wood and metal attachment. Her spirits soared as she wrapped her fingers around the familiar device.

"Yes you do. Here it is. Papa's latch!"

"Your Papa was the peddler who made this? If that's so, I owe him my life."

Mr. Prodan lifted her up onto the wagon and sat her down next to him. "But if he's gone, then I suppose I owe him your life." He stroked his beard. "This is troubling. I can't take you with me. I'm always on the road and these days it's too dangerous for anyone, let alone a child."

"Won't you help me, please?"

He thought for a moment. "There must be an orphanage in the city. I can take you to a Church—"

"Is there a synagogue?"

Mr. Prodan considered that. "There is a Jewish quarter. I can take you there. Perhaps they can help." He reached for her laundry, but Luska grabbed it first. She stowed it beneath the seat, close at hand, and held the beautiful tulip as he urged his horses forward.

Mr. Prodan's cart traveled through the streets at a steady pace. The rhythmic clip clop, clip clop of the horses steadied her nerves. The city seemed a lot less frightening to her now.

Street workers pressed their torches to gas lamps as dusk fell on the town. Curtains were being drawn in the townhouses they passed as lamps and candles were lit. Only a few people walked along the streets. The rest were home behind those glowing windows, eating supper...bowls of steaming broth with cabbage or onions, maybe some dumplings and slices of bread....

Luska heard her belly rumble. She couldn't remember the last time she had eaten a real meal, but thanks to Papa's latch, it might not be much longer. She thought about Mama's treasure, the precious goblet stowed inside her bundle, which led her to the florist shop where she met Mr. Prodan.

Wherever they were, Mama and Papa had managed to feed their daughter one more time.

Chapter Seven

Mr. Prodan stopped his cart in front of a large house where the caretaker of the synagogue had directed him to go. Even in the dark Luska could see lots of flowering bushes in the front yard. Mr. Prodan cradled her elbow as she climbed the steep steps leading to the door, her bundle wedged at her side, her other hand holding her tulip.

"Careful," he admonished. "Granite can be slippery."

Within moments a stately looking older man, dressed in a formal suit with white gloves, opened the door and, after hearing Mr. Prodan repeat the caretaker's instructions, invited them in. Except for a patch of gray hair over his lip, the older man was clean shaven and his head was uncovered.

Luska huddled against Mr. Prodan's leg. She whispered, "That man can't be a Rabbi."

"He's the butler, the manservant of the house."

The butler escorted them down a hallway with rooms on each side. Luska couldn't help but stare, as much in awe as enchantment. This house was much bigger than any she had ever seen, and more beautiful. The house had wood floors so clean they shined, and in every room, carpets as brightly colored as one of Mama's kerchiefs lay centered on the floor. They even had a rug on the stairway that reached up to another floor. There was an old rug in her synagogue, but she had never seen one in a home before.

Carved wood furniture, framed in gold, crowded every room. Statues, bowls and other delicate looking objects filled the tops of tables, chests and shelves. Luska wondered what purpose some of the beautiful things would serve. Dark beams ran along the length of the ceilings and paintings lined the walls. It all reminded her of stories Papa had told her about his dealings with rich merchants.

She stopped in front of a painting of a woman, young and beautiful, with large blue eyes, light brown hair framing her face, and skin as pale and pink as a baby's. She wore a gown the color of beets. There was something about the painting that made Luska want to stay there and look at it, but Mr. Prodan slipped his arm around her shoulder to urge her on.

The butler opened two side by side doors. "Would you kindly wait in the sitting room?"

Luska entered the room and turned in a circle, overwhelmed by the many wondrous items she saw. The colors in here were much softer, like the meadow in spring. She checked to see if anyone was watching her before she allowed her hand to brush against the gold trim around the arm of the sofa. To her surprise it did not feel cold like metal, but warm like wood.

Her feet had sunk into the patterned rug, the color of summer skies, with an oval of pale cream in the center, framed with pastel flowers that looked like they were carved into the thick pile. She couldn't resist squatting down to touch a flower until she heard a little giggle behind her. Luska bolted upright.

The butler had returned with a man finely dressed in a black jacket that reached his knees and pants that matched. He had dark eyes, a red beard, and stood taller than Papa, but not as filled out. Next to him stood the beautiful woman Luska had seen in the painting. She appeared older in person, but her face was still pretty. A ring of braids wrapped around her head. She had covered her hair with a kerchief, as a married woman would do. She wore a black dress with a skirt that flared out and fell in soft folds from a tight waistband, like an hourglass. The sleeves puffed out around her upper arms and narrowed down to her wrists. The women in the shtetl would have said she looked dignified. Luska liked her right away.

Peering through the doorway was a brown haired boy

around Luska's age, and a pretty blonde girl, no more than three, with a giggle that almost made Luska want to laugh, too.

The butler announced, "May I present Rabbi and Rebbetzin Zedek."

Mr. Prodan tipped his hat and introduced himself as the Rabbi led his wife to the sofa. The Rabbi nodded to Mr. Prodan and smiled pleasantly at Luska, but the boy glared at her with eyes like two burning lumps of coal.

"Welcome to our home." The Rabbi gestured to the chairs facing the sofa. "Please, make yourselves comfortable."

Luska glanced again at the fancy furniture and chose to stand. "Excuse me, could I have a glass of water, please?"

"Of course you may. Vostok, would you bring drinks for our guests?"

The butler returned shortly with a tray of filled glasses. He handed one to Luska. She took a few sips, then put her flower in the glass before placing it on the floor next to her bundle.

"Thank you."

Everyone stared at her. The little girl giggled again.

"Perhaps a bud vase would be in order. Vostok, would you...?" The Rebbetzin said. A flick of her hand was enough to tell the butler she wanted her children to leave with him.

Right before the door closed Luska heard the boy whisper to the butler, "Who is that dirty girl?" His sister answered back, "Ash girl, ash girl!" Luska felt her cheeks flush with humiliation. She smoothed her hair before picking up her possessions.

Mr. Prodan continued. "Allow me to present Lala. I found her wandering the streets earlier this evening."

She managed a small curtsy, which the Rebbetzin acknowledged with a quick smile.

"Why bring her to us, Mr. Prodan?"

"Several days ago..." he paused. "Lala, would you

49

please wait outside the room? I want to speak with the Rabbi and his wife alone."

The Rabbi's expression turned dark and his wife's smile vanished.

Luska's nerves set her stomach tumbling. "I want to be here with you, Mr. Prodan. Please, can't I stay?"

"No, it's best you leave us to talk privately."

She had trusted Mr. Prodan so far and couldn't think of a reason to stop now, but as she walked out of the room, each step became more difficult than the last.

Luska cast a lone shadow in the hallway. It vanished as the doors to the sitting room closed behind her. She pressed her ear to the crack between them and heard the Rebbetzin say, "Please continue, Mr. Prodan."

"Several days ago Cossacks attacked her shtetl. They razed the village and slaughtered everyone except her."

It was all true. Mr. Prodan remembered everything she had told him. Maybe it was because he was a salesman, or how he used grown-up words, but the way Mr. Prodan told the story—horrific spectacle, corpses, ghastly sights, wretched smells, terrifying nights—made it sound like it was happening once again, right now. As she listened, visions of her destroyed village swirled around her and flashed before her eyes. She shut them tight, shook her head to and fro, even pressed her hands over her face, all in a wasted effort to blot out the images.

She could hear screaming in her head. Luska turned her back to the door and covered her ears, desperate to make the nightmare stop. Her breath came short and rapid. She gazed up at the ceiling, longing to see Mama's face, praying to hear Papa's voice. Where were they? She chewed on her lip to keep from crying out. Would no one come to help her?

But hanging on the wall, watching over her with warm blue eyes, was the portrait of the Rebbetzin. Her face glowed with compassion and understanding, as though she could tell how much Luska was hurting. Luska stared into those blue eyes and imagined the woman's arms wrapped around her, stroking her hair and murmuring words of comfort. The scary images slowly faded away and soon were replaced by the smell of roasting meat and baking bread.

"...he left her in the city, which is where I found her." The door opened and Mr. Prodan guided her back into the bright sitting room.

The Rabbi stood as she entered. "My wife and I are well aware of the tragic implication of these attacks, Mr. Prodan. Many members of our congregation have taken in relatives orphaned in pogroms. It is an unfortunate situation for all concerned."

"I am confident that you will be able to help the child, Rabbi."

The Rabbi and his wife now looked at Luska with kind faces. The nightmare had passed. But when Mr. Prodan asked for his coat, she panicked.

"Please, Mr. Prodan, don't go yet."

"I must leave now if I am to get to the next town by tomorrow."

"But what will happen to me?"

Rabbi Zedek bent down and with gentle hands took hold of her shoulders.

"You can stay with us until we find you a new home, and we will. On that you have my word, Lala."

"And mine" added the Rebbetzin. "How astonishing that a young child like you could survive such an ordeal." A look of sorrow creased her face.

Several moments passed until the Rabbi cleared his throat, breaking the silence. "Naomi, dear, perhaps we...."

"Yes. Oh my, where are my manners. The child must be hungry." She cupped Luska's chin. "You should say goodbye to Mr. Prodan. Then I will have you washed up and into some clean clothes so you can join the children in the dining room."

Luska gave him a big hug.

"Thank you for helping me, Mr. Prodan. I'll never forget you."

"Goodbye, Lala. You will be safe now."

"So will you, thanks to Papa's latch."

He chuckled. "I am honored to have helped you, after what your Papa did for me. I feel certain you are in good hands now. Enjoy your life and remember what I told you — move forward and don't look back."

He tipped his hat, and was gone.

Chapter Eight

Luska reached out to the space where Mr. Prodan had been. The Rebbetzin clasped Luska's hand and held it as they left the sitting room together. Luska felt her heartbeat and breathing slow a bit, soothed by the touch of the beautiful woman whose portrait they now walked past. The Rebbetzin was as tall as Mama, but with a more rounded figure. Her soft hands and clean nails showed she didn't work much in the fields.

She led Luska to a tiny room with mops, buckets, cleaning rags and a broom. It also had a washbasin sunk into a stone counter atop a wood cabinet. Above the basin was another cabinet with metal doors that looked like dull mirrors.

Another woman, wearing a stiff white apron over a plain black dress, came in and filled the basin with hot water. She gave a nod as she helped Luska climb onto a wooden stepstool to reach the water more easily. The woman appeared to be younger than the Rebbetzin, with brown hair and dark blue eyes, but the skin on her hands felt rough, even rougher than Mama's.

The Rebbetzin inserted herself between Luska and the woman in the apron. "I shall bathe her, Anya."

Anya looked surprised. "Oh, I—"

"Bring some towels."

Anya nodded and left.

Luska caught her reflection in the shiny doors. She always took pride in keeping herself clean. Now a dirt-smudged face with matted hair stared back at her. She cringed at her appearance, made worse by her filthy clothes and shoes caked with mud. The children's taunts rang in her ears.

"Ash girl, ash girl"
"Who is that dirty girl?"

She moaned to the Rebbetzin, "Your boy was right, I am a dirty girl."

"Oh, dear child, pay no attention to Saul," the Rebbetzin said as she removed Luska's dress. "He is eight, and at that age boys like to tease girls. You cannot be more than five, but you will understand when you are older."

"I'll be eight when midsummer comes, after Mama's baby is...."

Luska caught her breath. She hadn't thought about the baby since the morning before the pogrom. Her stomach knotted as shame added to the pain. The Rebbetzin's face went white and although her lips moved, no words came out until she inhaled deeply.

"Let me make you presentable for dinner, and then I shall give you a proper bath after you have eaten." Her voice cracked as she spoke.

The Rebbetzin gently wiped Luska from head to toe with a sudsy washrag, taking extra care in cleaning her burned palm and skinned knees. The hot water felt good against her skin and the soap smelled like meadow flowers. It helped her put aside the horror of the past few days for a little while. Luska relaxed under the spell of the woman's touch.

The Rebbetzin kept looking at Luska's face and smiling, but sadness filled her eyes.

Anya carried in a stack of towels. She picked up Luska's dirty dress and then reached for her ball of laundry.

"No, don't take that away from me!" Luska shrieked. Frantic, she thrashed about and would have fallen off the stool had the Rebbetzin not grabbed her around the waist.

"Anya, leave it there."

The woman in the apron nodded to the Rebbetzin and left the room empty-handed.

Luska wriggled out of the Rebbetzin's grasp and

snatched her bundle.

"It's all I have."

"Of course, child, you may keep it with you."

Luska turned away from the Rebbetzin before loosening her ball of laundry. She pulled out her nightshirt and her blue dress and held them up.

"I have these to wear."

The Rebbetzin winced. "They need to be ironed. Anya," she called out. "Please have these...garments pressed, and bring something our young guest can put on in the meantime."

Anya returned for the clothing. "What would you like for her to wear, Madam?"

"Esther's clothes will be too small for her. Bring Saul's robe."

The Rebbetzin took Luska to a finely furnished room she first noticed upon entering the house, with a long table covered with a white cloth and laden with many silver and glass pieces. The Rabbi sat at the far end, and his wife took the seat opposite him. Saul and Esther sat together, their backs to a carved wooden cabinet with goblets and dishes stored behind its glass doors. Luska was seated across from them, her possessions on the empty chair beside her. She smiled at the children. Esther flashed a big grin before turning away. Saul, however, looked sour.

"Mother, why is she dressed in my robe," he pouted.

"She needs to wear it until her clothes are ready. Then you shall have it back."

Luska watched his eyes narrow and his lips draw together like they were basted with thread and pulled tight. If anyone else noticed, they did not speak of it.

She focused instead on the table. It had a sparkly bowl filled with flowers in the center, flanked by big silver candleholders the Rebbetzin had called candelabras. The place setting in front of her had a goblet, many spoons and forks, and dishes that all matched. Each had borders edged with curling gold lines, like a creeping vine, and tiny pink flowers on all the white parts. She touched one of the flowers. It felt raised, like it had been fastened on rather than painted. Luska didn't see any food, though. With everything else on the table, where would they put it?

Then Anya brought in a wide tray, which held a big covered bowl filled with soup and a loaf of bread on a wooden board. Luska counted three spoons by her plate; which one was supposed to be for soup?

After the Rabbi said the blessing for the bread, Anya served him first, but Luska noticed he waited until everyone's bowl was filled before he picked up the biggest spoon on the right side. She chose the same type to eat her soup.

"You have excellent table manners, Lala," his wife observed.

"Thank you, Rebbetzin," she murmured, avoiding Saul's icy stare.

After the soup came vegetables, meat and potatoes, and finally tea and cake. The Rebbetzin told her to eat as much as she wanted, but despite her hunger, she only managed half a bowl of soup before she lay down her spoon and sat quietly, barely able to follow the family's conversation. Saul continually shot glaring looks at her throughout the meal, but the warm room and a belly full of food left her too exhausted to care. Luska felt thankful when their mother excused the children from the table and sent them upstairs.

Anya gathered the dishes on a tray. "Madam, the girl's dresses are pressed."

"Wonderful. Go upstairs and prepare her bath."

The Rebbetzin helped Luska out of her chair. "I shall

give you a proper washing before we dress you in clean clothes. May I help you with your things?"

Luska nodded weakly. She could barely keep her eyes open. The Rebbetzin scooped Luska up from her chair and carried her upstairs to the bathing room. Luska placed her bundle near the bathtub, close at hand.

The tub had a dark gold waterspout attached to one end, with a handle on each side, but no pump for water. When Anya turned the handles, water rushed out all by itself, causing puffs of steam to rise over the surface of the tub. Luska gasped at the marvel before her.

The Rebbetzin rolled up a sleeve to her elbow and plunged her hand into the water. "It feels a little hot."

Anya turned one handle until the water slowed while her mistress fastened her sleeve around her wrist and took a moment to straighten her dress. Luska thought she looked like an empress in a palace. No wonder she named her children after a king and a queen.

"Anya, I want her dressed in a nightshirt. Would you bring one?" The Rebbetzin helped Luska into the bath and lathered her hair with a sweet smelling liquid.

As Luska soaked, her thoughts traveled back to her village. Every time she tried to picture her home, bad memories pushed away the good ones. She shook the nightmares out of her head and instead tried to focus on Mama and Papa, hoping to see their faces once more. She strained to hear their words of guidance, their stories, even their scolding, but nothing came forth. The open window presented only a starless sky.

Although the room was warm, a shiver ran through her. Luska hugged her knees close to her chest as unfamiliar hands soaped her back. She suddenly felt very alone without Mama and Papa. Her washtub at home might not pour its own water like this one, but Mama would be there to wash her. Tears mingled with the bath water flowing over her.

The Rebbetzin lifted her out of the tub and toweled her dry. "Oh dear, you are shivering." She retrieved Saul's robe. "Wear this until Anya brings your nightshirt." She helped Luska put it on. "Would you hold out your arms? I want to roll up the sleeves."

Luska obeyed, but kept her head down so the Rebbetzin wouldn't see her crying.

"Mama and Papa are gone," she sniffled, "they're really gone."

"It is very tragic, but you must not think about it." The Rebbetzin tried drawing Luska closer to tie the sash, but Luska stepped back.

"But you don't understand."

The sadness returned to the woman's eyes. "I do. Try to put it out of your mind."

"But I can't see them or hear them anymore."

"Yes, child, I know. Mr. Prodan told us what happened."

"He did? Then please tell me what happened to them. They've been with me all along until I came to your house," she whimpered. "Why have they gone away?"

Anya returned with Luska's nightshirt and laid it on the stool beside the tub.

The Rebbetzin held it up with two fingers. Her nose curled like she'd sniffed spoilt fish.

"Is this the best one she has?"

"It's the only one, Madam."

"Very well, Anya. Would you ask my husband to come here at once?"

Luska pulled her nightshirt over her head. The string ties at the neckline had been replaced with new yellow ribbons.

The Rabbi knocked before entering.

"Why look at you, child. You are even lovelier all cleaned up. Are you still hungry? You ate very little at dinner." He called out through the door, "Anya, bring up a small bowl of soup, and some bread, not too much though."

"Hershel, Lala is having some difficulties."

The Rabbi sat on the stool. "Lala, is something troubling you? Are you having bad memories of what happened to your village?"

"Sometimes… it's like it's happening all over again."

"I can only imagine how frightening it must be for you, but do not be concerned. The reason everything is coming back to you now is because you are in a safe place. If you can remember that, it may help you put it out of your mind."

"But I can't see or hear Mama and Papa anymore." Her eyes stung from soapy tears. "I still need them. Please, Rabbi, can't you do something so they'll come back to me?"

He gently patted her shoulder. "You have been through a terrible experience, child. You witnessed an unspeakable crime against your entire village, especially your family. I know you miss them very much and wish they were still here with you, but your Mama and Papa are gone."

"But why would they bring me here and then leave me?"

"Dear child, it was Mr. Prodan who brought you here."

"No, it was Mama and Papa," she insisted. "They've been with me all along. They came to help me when I was lost in the forest and showed me the right path to follow. Then when I reached the village, Papa told me how to find food and a ride to the city. And Mama's treasure led me to the flower shop and Mr. Prodan. But I can't see them or hear them now. Where did they go? Why won't they come help me anymore?"

The Rabbi looked puzzled. He turned to his wife, but she merely shrugged. His foot tapped on the small white tiles until he raised his finger to poke the air.

"Well, Lala, I think they wanted to guide you to a safe place, and now that you are here with us, their job is done. Their souls can rest, and you can go on without thinking about this anymore."

His wife nodded in agreement.

Anya stood in the doorway holding a tray. On it was a steaming bowl of soup and a small vase with Luska's yellow tulip.

"Madam, would you like this in the guestroom or one of the children's rooms?"

"Put it in the front bedroom."

The Rabbi and Anya both looked shocked. Luska thought she heard him gasp.

"Naomi, are you sure – "

"Yes, dear. Anya, get the room ready for tonight. Lala and I will be there shortly."

She picked Luska up in her arms and brushed a few stray hairs behind her ears. "Dear, would you tuck the children in tonight? I want to stay with her for awhile."

The Rabbi took Luska's hand between his. "I shall come back later, after you have eaten, and we can talk more about this." He gave his wife the strangest look, then kissed her on the cheek before he left.

The Rebbetzin set Luska down and took her by the shoulders. "You must put all your sorrows out of your mind," she instructed. "The sooner you stop thinking about what you have lost, the faster the pain will go away."

It took a while before the maid returned to the bathing room and informed them that the room was ready. When Anya opened the door, the Rebbetzin drew in a deep breath and hesitated before entering. Luska's nose curled a bit. It smelled a little stale and musty inside, like it did in her old hiding place under her house behind the stoop, but that didn't explain why the Rebbetzin looked distressed.

Luska wondered what was so unusual about the front

bedroom to cause the woman's face to tighten with every glance. It had a small bed, with one side pushed close to the wall and a nightstand with a lamp on the other side. Beneath the drapery-clad window sat a low chest of drawers. Anya had set her food on a low round table positioned in front of the chest, with a chair perfectly sized for Luska tucked underneath. Against the back wall was an overstuffed chair for a grown-up, flanked on one side with a second nightstand.

The Rebbetzin sat in that chair as she watched Luska eat. The strain in her face slowly melted away and in no time she wore the same expression she had in the painting.

Luska put her spoon down.

"Lala, if you are finished, come sit awhile with me."

She climbed onto the big chair next to the Rebbetzin and sank into its fluffy cushions. She tilted her head so the Rebbetzin could run a silver brush through her hair. Her body ached and exhaustion drained her strength. The Rebbetzin counted each stroke in a gentle song. The steady rhythm lulled Luska. Her eyelids would sink until they touched her bottom lashes and then bounce open.

The bed looked inviting, but Luska fought the desire to sleep. She gazed at her bundle, nestled against the bed pillow, and thought about what the Rabbi had told her. She couldn't believe her parents would no longer be there to help her. After all, the Rabbi said that she would only be staying with them until they could find her a new family. She felt sure Mama and Papa wouldn't go off and leave her until she had a new home and people to take care of her. They wouldn't do that. It just wasn't their way.

Chapter Nine

"…ninety eight, ninety nine, one hundred."

The Rebbetzin laid the brush down on the nightstand. Luska ran her hand over her damp hair, surprised by how soft it felt. Drowsiness crept through her, but she shook it off when Rabbi Zedek and Anya returned to the room. The maid removed the tray with her empty soup bowl and a few crusts of bread left on the rim in case anybody else wanted to eat them. He sat on the bed with the weary look of someone facing an unpleasant duty. Luska stiffened.

"It looks like you were able to eat a little more, Lala. I hope you enjoyed it."

"The soup was delicious, Rabbi. I ate it all up. I'm sorry I couldn't finish the bread."

"No, you did fine. You should settle down and digest your food before you go to bed. Naomi, would you join me for a moment?" He gestured toward the door with his head.

His wife left the door partway open as the two of them went into the hallway. Luska slipped off of the chair, tiptoed to the door, and watched through the crack as the Zedeks walked to the far end of the hallway to talk.

"It was good of you to sit with Lala. She seems calmer now," the Rabbi said to his wife.

"That is why she should not do anything that would encourage her to focus on what happened; no sitting *shiva.*"

"At her age it is not a requirement," the Rabbi noted.

"She has made no mention of bad visions since you spoke with her."

Luska expected the Rabbi would be happy to hear that, but his face crinkled into a frown.

"They will continue unless she can bury her past. How

many families do we know who have taken in relatives orphaned under the same circumstances? We have seen what happens – the nightmares, the odd behavior. It disrupts the entire household."

He stood with arms crossed, shaking his head. "I have considered every family in my congregation, hoping I could think of even one who might take her in, but none has come to mind. Perhaps you can persuade one of the wives."

"I can make a plea to the Sisterhood tomorrow," the Rebbetzin volunteered.

"Can you think of anyone else?"

His wife looked back at him with a pinched smile.

He cleared his throat. "Are you sure?"

"Absolutely," she snapped.

He nodded. "But I gave her my word."

The Rebbetzin took his arm. "Hershel, I want to keep her."

Luska's heart began to race.

"Us? No, we cannot do that."

"Why not?" She kept her grip on his arm. "We can afford it."

"Your money is not the issue. It would not be fair to our children, or to her. Did you see how our son reacted? We need to keep our attention on Saul and Esther right now."

"I think your congregation would be impressed if we adopted her."

"Quite the contrary. They might be offended if we took in a stranger when we never spoke of adopting one of their orphaned relatives. I know you mean well, my dear, but—"

She clasped her hands over her heart. "But look what she went through, and survived. This child is very special."

He held her face in his hands. "I understand why you want to do this, why you put her in the front bedroom—no, do not deny it."

"I know what you are thinking, but this is different. It

will not happen again, not with her. In spite of everything, she is alive. Lala is a remarkable child. And after everything I have been through, I deserve this."

"Naomi, you cannot change the past, and this is not the way to change the future. We will help her, but our children must come first."

She waved her hand like she was shooing away a fly. "She deserves it as well."

"I agree. I would hate to send her to an orphanage, but we cannot take in every waif that comes to our city. They are all special."

"Not like her."

"But they all deserve a family to love and care for them." He let out a long breath. "We shall have to consider other options. I can send word out to nearby congregations as well."

"Hershel, I still think it would be best for her if we keep her here, with us."

He threw up his hands. "Parents are not replaceable."

"And children are?"

He raised his finger to his lips.

"Can we agree to adopt her if nothing else works out?" she whispered.

Luska tensed, waiting for his answer.

"This is not the time to decide. We should wait until after the Sabbath." He took his wife's hand and held it between his. "Maybe something will come to us during our prayers."

As Luska backed away from the door, she caught sight of a dark figure hiding at the top of the stairs. Could it be Papa or Mama? Trembling, she peered once more through the crack. There was Saul, listening in on his parents' conversation as she had, his dark eyes staring through her.

Luska hurried to the chair and hopped up moments before the Rabbi and his wife returned to the room.

He helped her off the chair. "You must be exhausted. Time to go to bed now. We can talk again in the morning."

She walked slowly, stalling while she thought of what to do. "Excuse me, Rabbi, I was wondering, when is Sabbath?"

"Tomorrow is Friday, child."

She let go of his hand and flew to the Rebbetzin's side.

"I can help you prepare for the Sabbath, Rebbetzin." The words raced from her lips. "I always helped Mama...you can use our Sabbath tablecloth. It's beautiful. Let me show you."

"Not tonight, it is very late and time for you to go to bed." She picked Luska up and tucked her under the covers. "You should sleep peacefully here." She stroked Luska's cheek as she gazed at her, all warm and smiling, then bent down and kissed her forehead.

"Good night, Lala."

The Rabbi extinguished the lamp and escorted his wife from the darkened room, leaving the door half open.

Luska stretched out in the soft featherbed dressed in her nightshirt, with its new satin ribbons tied into pretty bows. Her freshly washed hair spilled across the pillow. Next to her lay her precious bundle. Only one thing was missing.

"Your Mama and Papa are gone….."

"…their job is done. Their souls can rest, and you can go on…."

She pressed her bundle against her. How can I go on without Mama and Papa, she thought. How could they leave me alone, without a home or a family, unless….

"Hershel, I want to keep her."

Luska rolled over to gaze once again at her tulip, resting in its vase on the nightstand next to her bed, and thought about the pretty woman with the blue eyes who had just kissed her goodnight.

Chapter Ten

Eerie sounds crept through the darkness. Luska hummed softly to drown out the noises haunting the forest, with Papa's shirt wrapped around her as much for comfort as for warmth. The moon began its descent and the woods quieted until all she could hear was the crunch of leaves beneath her feet.

The sound of running water urged her ahead. She slid through the brush looking for its source, but more dense growth blocked her way. Twigs scraped her hands and bit her arms, but she burrowed through the knot of branches until she found the stream. As she scooped a handful of water to her lips, she saw a dark form reflected on the stream's surface.

What could it be, she wondered, and tried to make out what was out there, but it remained shadowy and hidden. Then, from the empty blackness came two dark eyes, glowing like burnt embers, towering over her, moving toward her, closer, closer....

Luska bolted awake with a scream. Her heart pounded wildly and her chest heaved as she struggled to breathe. Sweat drenched her whole body. Despite everything that had happened in the past few days, she never felt as terrified as she did at this moment.

The Rabbi came running into her room.

"What happened, Lala?"

She tried to tell him but couldn't get the words out.

He lit the lamp and sat beside her. "You must have had a nightmare."

"Oh, Rabbi, it was horrible," she panted, still out of breath. "It was so dark, and there was this monster hiding in the forest, and it kept staring at me, and I couldn't make it go away."

"It must have seemed very frightening, but it was only

a dream. There are no monsters here." He stroked her head. "You are safe now; no one is going to harm you. Lie down and try to go back to sleep."

"I'm too scared, I don't think I could." She looked around the room. "Where is the Rebbetzin?"

He exhaled. "Your nightmare scared the children. I hope she is with them."

"How many families do we know who have taken in relatives orphaned under the same circumstances? We have seen what happens – the nightmares, the odd behavior. It disrupts the entire household."

Luska broke into tears. "I'm sorry I bothered you. I'll be quiet now, I promise."

"You need not worry," he said softly. "The bad dream is over. You are a brave little girl, Lala. Now close your eyes and soon you will be asleep."

The Rabbi put out the lamp and left the room. Luska lay in bed, eyes wide open, too frightened to sleep. How could Mama and Papa leave her like this? She reached across the bed to her bundle and held it tightly against her as she wept.

She lay still for a long time, wanting to give in to exhaustion but afraid of what could happen if she fell asleep. Everywhere she looked, things that appeared ordinary in the light now took on threatening shapes in the darkened room. Moonlight snaked in between the curtains, casting scary shapes, throwing them against the wall...and the back of the chair. The little chair where she'd sat earlier, eating her supper, didn't seem to be a chair with two dowels on each side of the chair back anymore. No, in the dark, it looked like a wolf, with its ears pointed up, ready to catch the sound of prey and attack! She tensed and bit her lip over and over until a warm droplet of blood leaked onto her tongue. Would this night ever end?

She heard a creak coming from the hallway, then another. She caught her breath. Maybe it was the Rabbi, or his wife coming to check on her, or maybe...she gripped her bundle tightly to her. The creaking stopped. She heaved a sigh as the house fell silent once more.

The bedroom door opened slightly, then a little more.

"Rebbetzin, is that you?" she whispered nervously, hoping she guessed right.

No response.

The door opened a little more, then more creaking.

Her body trembled.

A small dark figure stood by the foot of the bed.

"Who...who's there," she stammered.

"Why did you come to my house?" The voice was low, small and ice cold.

Saul.

Luska sat up. "I had no place else to go."

"I do not like you and I do not want you here. You want to take her away from me, but you cannot have her."

"I don't understand." Why did he hate her so?

He marched over to the side of the bed and shook his finger in her face. "She is my mother, not yours. I will not let you take her from me!"

Luska froze, frightened and confused by the boy's anger. Saul stood his ground for a moment before backing off toward the door.

Before he left the room he turned to her and hissed, "I hope you die, too."

Chapter Eleven

Luska stared at the gap between the curtains as she waited for sunrise to end the long night. Fear of another nightmare, or visit from Saul, had kept her awake, so when the black sky took on a purple glow, she put on her gray dress, which Anya had washed and pressed. It felt as stiff as the dining room tablecloth. She pulled the covers over the mattress, tugged and smoothed them many times, but could not get the bed to look like it did last night. After trying her best she sat on the little chair, her ball of laundry on the table, and waited for someone to come get her.

No one came.

The sun was up now but the house remained quiet. She squirmed in her seat, stood up and sat down, and squirmed some more, all in time to a rhythmic tapping sound that turned out to be her fingertips drumming on the tabletop. She returned to the bed and fussed with the covers several times until it looked a little better, but still not as good as she would have liked, so she tried once more without success. Discouragement fed her uneasiness. She returned to the chair. No one had given her any chores yet, so what was she to do? Again she rose and circled the table, brushing her fingertips across the top of the small chest with each pass. She squatted down to examine the little pictures painted on the knobs. They looked like jumping rabbits.

She listened for footsteps or voices, but the house remained silent. She pulled open one of the dresser drawers. Inside were clothes that looked almost new. She held up a jacket of dark blue velvet, the same fabric as the Torah cover in her synagogue. Beneath it was a pair of matching pants and a glossy white shirt with a milky stain across the front. Clothes for a boy, but too small for Saul.

Muffled footsteps in the hall could be heard through the door. Luska closed the drawer and, with her possessions tucked under her arm, wandered into the deserted hallway.

Anya emerged from the bathing room carrying a basket of towels. She seemed startled to find Luska standing there.

"Good morning, Miss. I didn't think you'd be awake yet."

Luska followed the maid down the hallway.

"But it's daylight. There must be many chores to do in a big house like this."

"Yes, there are. Since you're already up, I'll tend to your room first."

Anya went into the bedroom where Luska had slept and paused at the bed.

Luska patted the covers. "I tried and tried, but I couldn't get it right. But if you show me how to do it, I could do a much better job next time."

"That's not necessary, Miss. I make all the beds."

Luska cradled her bundle to her chest. "I'm sorry, did I do something wrong?"

Anya ran her hand over the covers. "Not at all. That was...thoughtful. But you must be hungry. Why don't you come downstairs and I'll serve you breakfast."

Luska stood at the top of the stairs. The rail was too high for her to reach firmly, and the lower floor was a long way down. Anya took Luska's hand and walked at her pace, one slow step at a time.

"Madam, don't the Rabbi's children do chores?"

"No, Miss. Vostok and I maintain the household."

"Just the two of you do all the chores in this big house? Your mama and papa must be very proud of you."

"I suppose so." Anya released Luska's hand as they cleared the bottom step.

72

"Thank you for washing and ironing my dress, Madam." Luska twirled around. "You did a very good job getting all the mud and leaves out. You can hardly tell it's the same one I wore yesterday."

"Why...thank you, Miss."

"You're welcome, Madam. I've never seen you smile before now. You look so pretty when you do." She headed for the dining room.

"No, Miss, that's not where the family has breakfast. They eat in the breakfast room."

"You have one room for eating breakfast, and another one for eating dinner? Oh my, no wonder this house is so big."

Anya walked her to the room nearest the staircase. A large gold-framed mirror hung on the wall. To its left were two dark wood doors with a window in each of them.

Luska began to unravel her ball. "Would you take some of my laundry?"

"I'd be happy to clean anything you need, Miss."

"It's already clean. I want you to take some of it in trade for my supper last night, and breakfast. Oh, and the room, too."

"That's not necessary."

"But it is, Madam. I have no coins to pay you, and if I can't do chores to earn my food and shelter, I have to trade for it. Otherwise it would be taking charity, and my Mama and Papa said not to do that, it's not our way."

Anya opened the doors to the breakfast room. "But having you here is not really charity. You've been invited to stay. You're a welcome guest, so you should feel like one of the family. Alright?"

Luska nodded. She knew a guest would have a meal or stay for a while, but they usually brought some food with them, or helped with the chores. If she kept asking to help, like she did with Mama and Papa, maybe the Zedeks would eventually say yes, too.

"Now, what would you like to eat, Miss?"

"Tea, please, and bread if you have it."

"What kind of bread do you like?"

"I like it best when it's not too stale, but I'll eat any bread you have, Madam."

Anya chuckled. "Fine, Miss, I'll be right back with an assortment, and you can choose whatever pleases you."

The breakfast room was as long as it was wide, with walls the color of a winter sky and a hard floor that looked like flat pebbles floating in a sea of cream. A simple round wood table with a smooth top sat in the center of the floor. Hanging above it was a plain gold metal lamp with six curved arms. More light shone through glass panels in the doors and the three-sided windows that pushed out from the back wall. Along one side stretched a narrow corridor that led to a flight of steps that Anya had just walked down. A wooden cart with dishes stacked on its lower shelf pressed against the corridor's outer wall.

Luska sat near the windows, which overlooked a large back yard carpeted in short grass and edged with bushes and a few trees. A patch of cheery white flowers filled one corner. The other side had been dug up but lay fallow. Beyond it stood a high stone wall that blocked her view of the sky.

The Rabbi carried his newspaper into the breakfast room. "Good morning, Lala. You seem to have slept well." He took the chair facing her.

Luska heard footsteps approaching from the back stairs. Anya carried up a large tray filled with dishes and baskets to the waiting cart. She transferred a pink and green floral teapot, a basket filled with bread, butter in a dish, several jam jars, and a platter with cheese to the top shelf before wheeling the cart into the room. Luska eyed the bounty as the maid draped a napkin across the Rabbi's lap and spread a cloth over the table before setting the food at its center. From beneath the cart she removed silverware, plates, and three cups that matched the teapot. She set each cup on a small dish and filled two with tea, which she placed near the Rabbi and Luska, then waited by the door.

The Rebbetzin entered with her children. She wore a white dress of a fabric that gleamed like it had been polished, with lace ruffles around her throat and down the center of her bodice. She sat next to her husband and placed Esther beside her. Saul's eyes bored into Luska.

"Mother, that girl is sitting in my seat!"

"You can have it back tomorrow."

Pouting, Saul took the seat next to his father.

Mindful of how she disturbed everyone's sleep last night, Luska said "Good morning" as cheerfully as possible. Esther flashed a grin, and then looked away shyly, but Saul sulked in his chair, just like yesterday. Luska turned hopefully to the Rabbi and his wife.

The Rebbetzin looked pale. When Anya put a plate in front of her, she waved it away. "Only tea for me." She looked across the table at Luska. "What are you drinking?"

"It's tea, Madam," Anya responded. "The child asked for it."

"She is too young to be drinking tea. Take that away and bring her a glass of milk."

Anya whisked the cup away from the table. Luska was about to say Mama always gave her tea in the morning, but decided it would be impolite. Anya poured glasses of milk for the children.

"Anya, would you mind serving breakfast? I do not believe I can manage it today."

"Yes, Madam."

Luska shrank back in her chair and chewed her lip. Waking everyone up last night was a very bad thing to do, and now the Rebbetzin wasn't feeling well because of it.

Anya made up plates with small wedges of cheese and buttered bread topped with jam. She served the Rabbi and

Esther before making up plates for Saul and Luska.

"Butter and jam together. What a feast!" Luska exclaimed. The Rebbetzin smiled weakly, but the children just stared at her. She caught Saul glowering at her plate. Her serving was slightly larger than his. She slumped back into her chair and quietly finished her meal. Anya promptly filled her empty plate with more buttered bread. She leaned over and whispered in Luska's ear, "Put your napkin on your plate when you're done."

The Rabbi disappeared behind his newspaper. "Dear, what are your plans for today?"

"I have to meet with the Sisterhood later this morning." The Rebbetzin sighed. "I should also find some clothes for Lala before the Sabbath."

"Excuse me, Rebbetzin, but I have all my clothes here." Luska held up her bundle.

"Yes, but you need proper clothes."

"What do you mean by 'proper'?"

"Something nice and new, more suitable for the city. As you can see," she gestured toward her children, "we dress more formally here, and we would like you to fit in."

The Rabbi put his newspaper down. "I want to bring Saul to the synagogue with me today. Mr. Grossfleisch will be in."

The Rebbetzin perked up. "The millionaire? Why not invite him and his wife for Sabbath dinner? His wife told me he likes goose."

"Excellent idea. Get Vostok and Anya working on it right away." He kissed his wife's cheek. "I shall try to be home early. Come, Saul."

Luska finished her bread and left her napkin on the plate. Anya gave her a small nod before she took the place setting away. Esther sang quietly to herself while her mother leaned back in her chair and stared into space.

"Rebbetzin, can I help you with some chores today?"

The Rebbetzin gave her a real smile. "No child, there is nothing you need to do. Would you like to play with Esther?" She got up, leaving half her tea in the cup. She whispered to Anya, "Keep an eye on them" before she left.

Luska watched Esther amuse herself as Anya cleared the table. The child swung her legs in time to her song as she rolled bits of bread into peas with her tiny fingers. Her blonde curls danced as she rocked in her chair. She looked sweet in her pink dress. It had a sheer apron over a floral print fabric, all edged with white lace. The yellow dress Esther wore yesterday was pretty, too. Luska looked down at her own dress. It was clean, but it was also worn and faded. It would be nice to have a new dress as pretty as Esther's to wear on the Sabbath, but maybe that would be taking charity. Mama and Papa wouldn't like that. She wished the Zedeks would allow her to do chores, but if not, she would have to think of another way to repay them.

Esther's big brown eyes fixed on Luska. She slipped out of her chair and grinned broadly, revealing almost as many empty spaces as teeth. "Ash girl, ash girl."

"Please don't call me that, Esther. I had my bath last night."

The little girl tugged on Luska's hand, urging her out of the chair. She pointed to the stairway, continuing her chant of "ash girl, ash girl."

"Alright, I'll follow you, but please call me Lala. I'm not an ash girl."

With hands linked, Esther led her upstairs, down the hallway and into her bedroom.

Esther's white bedroom furniture was unlike anything Luska had ever seen. The bed, painted with pink and gold flowers, had four poles rising up from the corners, with a sheet of white lace draped over the top like a chupa canopy at a wedding. Esther searched through shelves, filled with toys that looked like children and animals, until she found a book.

"Ash Girl." Esther handed it to her, pointing to its cover. It showed a drawing of a girl sleeping on the floor next to an open hearth.

"I can't read, Esther."

The child opened the book.

Luska leafed through it, studying the illustrations that appeared on every page. The pictures told a story about a girl who lived with a woman and two other girls. The others wore nice dresses, but the poor girl dressed in rags. Luska paused at the drawing in the center of the book, which covered two pages. It showed a village celebration, with everyone dressed up in fancy gowns and suits. In the background was the biggest, tallest, most beautiful house she had ever seen, with many pointed towers, curved walls and balconies, sitting on top of a hill overlooking the village.

Esther pointed to the house. "Prince."

Luska turned the page. Somehow the poor girl had changed into a lovely young woman, dressed in a beautiful gown and shoes. She went into the big house where a handsome man danced with her. Then she ran away, leaving her shoe behind.

Luska closed the book and gave it back to Esther. "You thought I was the girl in the story. I'm sorry I scolded you, but look at me." She turned around in a circle. "I'm all clean now. I'm not an ash girl anymore."

"No more!" Esther squealed in delight.

Luska couldn't help but smile.

The child returned to her own game. She plunked her doll on the bed. "Go nap nap dolly. Make shush shush. No wake Momma."

Mama.

Mama might have had the baby by now. Would it have been a little girl, like Esther, so charming and giggly? Or maybe a boy who would grow up to help Papa carve latches, or even become a peddler? Luska welled up. She sat on the floor and hugged her knees to her chest.

"No cry baby," Esther scolded.

Embarrassed, Luska wiped away her tears before realizing that Esther was talking to her doll. Crying, nightmares…when would it end?

"The reason everything is coming back to you now is because you are in a safe place."

Safe from the forest, from hunger, but without that to worry about, all she had left was sadness about the past and emptiness about her future.

The Rebbetzin took his arm. "Hershel, I want to keep her."

Luska's heart began to race.

"Us? No, we cannot do that."

"Why not?" She kept her grip on his arm. "We can afford it."

"Your money is not the issue. It would not be fair to our children, or to her. Did you see how our son reacted? We need to keep our attention on Saul and Esther right now."

She appeared to have won over the young girl as well as her mother. If only she could think of a way to get Saul to like her, maybe her future would be clearer.

Chapter Twelve

The two girls spent the morning at play. Esther had strewn most of her toys across the bedroom floor. Luska thought about straightening up, but she remembered that Anya did that. Although it felt odd not to be doing any chores, Luska decided watching over the child was one way to repay the Zedeks for their kindness. Seeing the girl having fun also eased some of Luska's sorrow.

Esther popped her Jack-in-the-Box for the tenth time when Anya called through the door.

"Lunch is ready."

"Lunch?" asked Luska.

"The midday meal. Don't you eat lunch?"

Luska shook her head. "No, Madam, just breakfast and supper."

Anya shrugged. "Why don't you try it? And you don't have to call me 'Madam,' my name is Anya."

"Oh, I couldn't. Mama taught me I shouldn't call grown-ups by their first name. May I call you Miss Anya instead?"

"Yes, Miss."

"Then you can call me Lala."

"It wouldn't be right to call a guest by name, Miss," she explained as she took the girls downstairs.

Vostok, the butler, was kneeling at the front door, polishing the golden metal parts until they gleamed. He looked different today, for instead of his formal black coat, he wore an apron over his white shirt which she imagined was as stiff as her dress had been.

"Good day, sir," Luska called out. "Thank you again for letting me in last night."

"You're very welcome, Miss." He returned to his polishing.

"You must be a very important person here, sir, to be allowed to touch the gold."

He gave her a curious look over his shoulder. "It is brass I'm polishing, not gold."

"Really? You've made it look so shiny I thought it must be gold."

Vostok looked at her, then at Anya. Anya just shrugged.

"You did a very good job shining the brass in the inside-out house, too."

At this he turned around to face her. "Beg pardon, Miss?"

"Where I took my bath."

"Oh, of course, an inside outhouse." Anya nodded. "It's called a 'toilette.'"

"Twa...LET?"

"That's it, Miss."

"There are so many wonderful things in this house, but I think I like that room the best. If you ever spent a winter in my village, you'd know why."

Vostok cleared his throat. "The inside outhouse. Very good."

"Let's leave Vostok to his work and go have our lunch." Anya suggested.

Luska looked around. "Where is the lunch room?"

"Lunch room?"

"Yes, Miss Anya. You have a breakfast room for eating breakfast and a dining room for eating dinner. Don't you have a lunch room for eating lunch?"

Vostok let out a chuckle.

Anya ushered the girls to a side door near the dining room. "Poor dear, all this must be so confusing for you. But you've given me an idea. It's a lovely day. Why don't you and

Esther have your lunch in the garden?"

"Aren't you and Mr. Vostok going to eat with us?"

Anya's sunny expression faded.

"No, Miss, Vostok and I don't eat with the family or their guests. It's not proper."

"But you're wearing very nice clothes. Isn't that what the Rebbetzin said 'proper' means?"

"What I mean is, it's just not done, that's all." Anya opened the door to the back yard, but Luska remained inside.

"Where do you eat?"

"In the kitchen, downstairs."

"But you cook the food, and clean the house, and do all the chores. Why can't you eat with the family?"

Anya looked serious. "Vostok and I are in service. We maintain the household. We take care of the Rabbi's home in exchange for room and board, meals and a place to stay, that is, plus a small allowance. We're not members of the family, we're employees. Laborers. Do you understand?"

Luska nodded. She understood the words, but not the idea that hard-working people could be treated like that. It went against everything Mama and Papa had taught her.

Chapter Thirteen

Luska was on the second floor when she heard the front door open. She looked down as the Rebbetzin rushed in, sounding winded. She wore a cloudy blue dress with a bell shaped skirt that puffed out in the back, and a matching short jacket with the most beautiful embroidery Luska had ever seen. Her hair was tucked so carefully into a hat covered with flowers that not one strand had fallen out.

Anya met her at the door.

"How are the preparations for dinner, Anya?"

"Everything is underway, Madam."

The Rebbetzin drew a deep breath. "Excellent. At least something is going well."

Anya took her hat. "Is there something I can help you with?"

"Not unless you can pry open the hearts of the Sisterhood." She peeled off her ivory gloves. "I cannot understand it. You would think after hearing what that poor child went through, they would have more pity, but instead, they went on and on about their orphaned relatives. My husband was right. When I mentioned we were considering adopting her, not one could fathom why we would endeavor to save this child, a complete stranger, when there are so many…where is she now?"

Luska backed away from the landing.

"Upstairs with Esther, Madam. The two girls are getting along very well."

"Yes, I expected that. Esther seemed quite taken with her this morning. Of course, Saul is a different matter."

"Do you have any packages for me to bring in?"

"Packages? Oh, you mean for the child. I am

embarrassed to admit it, but I allowed the women to talk me out of buying her clothes. Mrs. Grossfleisch actually suggested we take some things for her from the Temple's poor box. 'That is its purpose,' she says. I could not bring myself to do that, but I felt too tired to argue, so I left empty-handed." She rubbed her forehead. "I still feel tired. I think I shall lay down for a nap. Would you see that I am not disturbed for an hour?"

"Yes Madam."

"Have my wine red dinner gown pressed – no, Mrs. Grossfleisch has seen me in that one. I shall wear the dove gray dress instead."

"With the bolero jacket, Madam?"

"Not that dress, the taffeta with the black plastron and velvet ribbons. Lay out the matching shoes and my thin white gloves. I want to wear my good pearls as well; Mrs. Grossfleisch favors her rubies. And have Vostok set up the dining room for four and the breakfast room for three. The Grossfleischs prefer to dine without children present. Let them have their dinner before sundown and then join us for the candle lighting."

Luska darted into her room before the Rebbetzin could see her. When she heard the door close down the hall, she sank into the bed.

"You're a welcome guest, so you should feel like one of the family".

But she wasn't one of the family.

"You would think after hearing what that poor child went through, they would have more pity...."

Hearing that no one at the Sisterhood wanted her was disappointing, until she remembered that someone else did.

The Rebbetzin took his arm. "Hershel, I want to keep her."

"Us? No, we cannot do that."

"Why not?"

Why not indeed.

If no one else wanted her, the Zedeks couldn't send her

away. She would have to stay here a little longer. That would be agreeable to her. She liked it here, where it was warm and safe. She liked Miss Anya and Mr. Vostok. She liked the Rabbi and his wife, even Esther.

"Of course, Saul is a different matter."

Saul. He'd been her biggest enemy in the house. Now she needed to turn him into a friend. The question was how?

Luska fastened the last button on her blue dress when Anya knocked on the door.

"Miss, I have some new clothes for you." She held up two dresses. "The family is entertaining very important guests tonight, and you'll want to look your best. Which would you like to wear at dinner—the yellow dress, or the blue one with pink rosebuds?"

"I want to wear my own dress tonight, thank you."

"You don't like either of them?"

"They're very pretty, but I already have clothes. So thank you, but I couldn't take either dress unless I can find a way to repay the Rabbi for them. I'll be sure to thank him for his kindness, though."

"You'll have to thank Saul, then. When he learned his mother did not...have any dresses for you, he wanted to help. He picked them out especially for you."

"Saul did?" Luska's jaw dropped in shock. The dresses were lovely, as nice as any Esther had worn, but she already owed the Zedeks so much. What would Mama and Papa think about this?

Mama crossed her arms. "Take something without working for it? No Luska, that would be charity, and we don't take charity."

They wouldn't like it. Mama wouldn't take meat from Mr. Chelmsky, and he was family.

But if Saul bought them for her, it would hurt his

87

feelings if she turned them down. He'd be angry, and maybe the Zedeks would send her away to make him happy.

Her stomach boiled and she chewed on her lip. She should say no, thank you, but...

"Miss, why don't you try one on before you decide?"

Her head fell in shame, but she nodded.

Anya helped her out of her clothes and slipped the blue dress over her head. Although the length was perfect, the dress was big enough for two Luskas. Her arms fell through the puffy sleeves like clappers in a bell.

"My goodness, I'll have to take this in at least ten centimeters. Let's try the other one."

The yellow dress was also too big for her tiny frame, but it fit a little better.

Luska turned to Anya, tears flowing down her cheeks. "Do you think Saul would be pleased if I wore one of these dresses?"

The maid dabbed away Luska's tears with the corner of her apron. "I suppose so, Miss. I believe we can fix this up enough for you to wear tonight."

Anya left, but soon returned with her sewing basket and a drawstring bag filled with ribbons. She found a wide yellow piece long enough to wrap around the high waistband and tie behind in a bow. Then she cut a piece of white ribbon, folded it in half lengthwise, and coiled it around until it looked like a small flower. She ran a needle and thread through it to firm up the shape, and with a few quick stitches, attached it to the ribbon and the dress. Finally, she cut a length of yellow ribbon for Luska's hair. Anya stood back to admire her handiwork.

"What do you think, Miss?" She held up a small mirror.

The dress fit better now, and the ribbons Anya added looked pretty. She chewed her lip. What would Mama and Papa say? After all, she had two dresses, maybe not as nice or as new as these, but they were hers. Mama and Papa would say taking charity is not their way. Oh, but if it could help to win Saul over....

She sighed, "I will wear this dress tonight."

Chapter Fourteen

Luska walked down the stairs, reminding herself with each step that no matter what Saul did to upset her, she would be nice to him. Even if he said something mean, she would close her ears and behave, like Mama taught her. Then maybe he would like her. He had to, for she felt certain the only way she could stay with the Zedeks was to win over Saul.

She rubbed her knuckles to make the throbbing go away; she had squeezed the banister so tightly her fingers ached. Pausing for a moment before entering the breakfast room, she caught a glimpse of herself in the hallway mirror. The finely dressed girl who looked back was almost unrecognizable.

"Are you ready for dinner, Miss?" Vostok stood behind her.

She nodded. "Excuse me, sir. Do I look...proper...for dinner?"

"More than proper, you look lovely, Miss." He tipped his head to her.

She accepted the compliment with flushed cheeks and a bashful smile. With one deep breath for courage, she entered the breakfast room.

Saul and Esther were already seated. Esther beamed when she saw Luska, while Saul, eyebrows raised, appeared full of himself. Luska took another deep breath as Vostok drew the sliding doors closed, leaving the children alone.

"Good Sabbath, Esther. Good Sabbath, Saul."

The front half of the table had been set. Esther and Saul sat facing each other, so Luska took the open chair between them and placed her napkin across her lap, as she had been taught to do. The curtains had not been drawn and the late day sun cast a golden glow on the back stone wall. She bit her lip before turning to Saul.

"Thank you for bringing the dresses for me, Saul. It was very kind of you, and I wish to repay your kindness someday."

Her hope that Saul would accept her gratefulness with appreciation was not met. His sly grin and rolling eyes spoke even if he didn't—he held back a secret like a bug hidden between his palms.

"Father expects me to do a good deed every Sabbath." He grinned. "Do you know where I got them?"

"It doesn't matter where they came from. What matters is the kindness you've shown me."

"Maybe next week I can bring you some shoes."

Esther extended her leg. "Shoes." She pointed to hers.

"Yes, Esther, those are your shoes." Luska smiled. "They're very pretty."

"Pretty!" the little girl repeated. She pointed at Luska. "You pretty. Ash Girl all gone."

"That's right. Ash Girl is all gone, thanks to your parents...and Saul."

Esther looked around. "Where Momma and Poppa?"

Saul draped his napkin across his lap. "They are dining with the Grossfleischs tonight, so we have to eat in here. Rich people don't dine with their children."

"But you eat with your parents, and you're rich."

Saul gawked at Luska.

"Us? Rich? Ha!"

"But your big house, with so many rooms filled with wonderful things."

"We are not rich, not compared to the Grossfleischs. Their house is so much bigger than ours, with many, many servants, more than you can count. They even have servants who work in the garden, or the stable. They have more rooms than us, more furniture, more everything. When I grow up, I want to have a big house and lots of money like the Grossfleischs, and be the richest man in the world."

Anya carried in a tray with three little plates, each with a small mound of something brown and pasty. It had a strong smell, like liver, but it didn't look like the liver Mama made, chopped up into chunks with boiled eggs and lots of fried onions.

A loud crash echoed from downstairs.

"What was that," cried Saul.

"Oh, dear! That can't be good. I must go downstairs right away. Miss, could you help the little one with her food until I can return?"

"I will."

Anya hurried down the stairs, leaving the children alone and staring at each other.

"What should we do?" Luska asked.

"I am hungry. I say we should eat now." Saul started for his plate, but withdrew his hand instead. "No, you begin, Lala."

He was up to something, but she was determined not to be drawn into a fight. She remembered how Mama always used flattery to butter up the vain Mrs. Radovich.

"Since your father isn't here, you're the man of the house. You should begin."

"Yes, but you are our guest, so you should begin."

Luska's heart pounded. "But last night, the Rabbi —"

Saul shook his finger at her. "I saw what you did last night. You had no idea which silverware to use, so you waited to see what my father would do, and then you did the same thing. You even fooled Mother into thinking you had excellent table manners, but I do not believe it. So, I am not going show you what to do." A mean grin spread across his face as he sank back into his chair and crossed his arms. "You said you would help Esther – I want to see how good your table manners really are."

93

Luska wished she could disappear. Saul had set a trap and she fell right in. She stared at the plate in front of her, surrounded by forks, spoons and knives. How could she tell which piece to use when she didn't know what she was eating? The round spoon looked too big, but perhaps the smaller spoon to its right? She reached out to it in slow motion, but as her fingers neared the handle, she heard him snicker. She yanked back her hand as though it had been burned.

"Wrong! Try again," he proclaimed.

She looked over the pieces again, this time focusing on the three forks. She thought about the smaller one to the left, which looked exactly like the fork above her plate. Her stomach knotted up as she sensed Saul's eyes burning through her. She held the plate by its rim and turned it in a circle, looking for a clue. Her finger poked the side of the mound. It felt soft and moist, like soaked bread. She withdrew her hands and laid them in her lap, under the table, where he couldn't see her grab and twist her napkin.

Saul snickered again. "You were going for that fork, I could tell, but you are wrong, wrong, wrong."

Luska fumed, but she refused to let him see how much he upset her. She looked toward Esther, who quietly sang to herself. And she promised to help the child eat.

Saul leaned toward her. "Get out of that bedroom and go back to your village, with your rags and your dirty face and your low class manners," he jeered. "That bedroom is being saved for someone worthy, and if I do not deserve it, then you certainly do not."

She sprung from her chair like an angry lion and fought her anger, which roared just as loudly.

"I understand why you want to do this, why you put her in the front bedroom...."

"Lala is a remarkable child...she deserves it...."

94

Saul was wrong. Calmed by the Rebbetzin's words, Luska sat down.

"Lala has a temper, ha ha, ha ha, and I made her lose it, ha ha...."

His bratty taunts sent her fury raging out of control—if Saul wanted to laugh at her, she'd give him something to laugh about.

She picked up the small knife. With it she scraped up a bit of the paste and with one bold swipe, spread the liver on her tongue. She turned to Saul; his eyes wide, mouth open. She shocked him. Now what?

Luska winced. Her hotheaded behavior led her to do the wrong thing. Saul's face twisted up into a knot and he began to quiver. She pushed back against her chair and dug her nails into the seat, unsure if he would yell, or throw something, or burst apart like an overcooked potato.

And then his face broke out in a joyous grin and he laughed. Not like when he mocked her, but a real laugh, a squeaky high laugh that sounded like a little girl giggling. He rocked back and forth in his chair and laughed so hard, tears streamed down his face.

"That was funny, do...ha ha...do it again!" he managed to say between fits of giggles.

She slid more liver on her tongue, and he collapsed into laughter once more, holding his stomach as he wriggled in glee. Luska laughed, too.

Saul playfully poked her arm. "My turn now. Watch me, watch me." He lifted his knife and painted his tongue and lips with the liver, then turned to the girls and made a silly face.

Esther and Luska burst out laughing, and Saul did, too. None of them could stop.

Luska felt tears bubble in her eyes, tears of happiness. Tears of relief.

At last, she thought, Saul likes me!

"Me, me!" Esther took her knife and dabbed a small pile of the brown paste on the tip of her tongue, which she stuck out for all to see. That set them off giggling once again, especially when the pellet of liver rolled out of her mouth and fell plop onto the child's lap. Her surprised look amused them even more, and they kept laughing so hard that they didn't hear Anya coming up the stairs until she dropped her tray of challah loaves. The two braided egg breads rolled across the floor.

The maid's hands flew to her face. "Oh my! What are you doing?" Her eyes darted from one child to another until they locked on Esther's brown-smudged face.

Esther showed her by spreading a huge mound of liver across her tongue, which she wiggled and shook, flicking dots of brown onto the tablecloth.

At that moment the sliding doors opened and there stood the Zedeks with a fat woman and an even fatter man – the Grossfleischs.

Anya, Saul and Luska froze, but Esther turned to the grown-ups. Waving her knife in the air, she presented her brown-coated tongue with a loud "aaahhhhhh."

"What is this?" the Rabbi cried.

"What...what are you children doing?" His wife looked even paler than she did at breakfast. .

"Eating, Momma," offered Esther, sticking out her tongue to prove her point.

"Anya, how could you let this happen?"

"I'm very sorry, Madam, I had to tend to the kitchen. I just got here myself." She picked up the fallen tray, but kept her head down.

The Rebbetzin scooped Esther up in her arms and wiped her face with a napkin. "Saul, what is going on here? Why are you eating in such an uncivilized manner? Your father and I taught you better than this!"

Saul put on an innocent face. "Please, Mother, do not

96

be angry with me. Esther and I know our table manners, but when Lala started eating like that, we thought it would be rude not to use our knives like she did. We did not want to make her feel ashamed."

"That was thoughtful of you, Saul." As she said it, he threw a smug grin at Luska.

"Mr. Grossfleisch, Mrs. Grossfleisch, please forgive the children," the Rabbi explained with a weak smile. "They are usually very well behaved, but they are not used to dining without adult supervision."

Luska saw a chance to be helpful. "Why couldn't Miss Anya and Mr. Vostok eat with us? They're adults."

Mr. Grossfleisch chuckled. His thick neck, which hung from his chin to his chest like a big coin pouch, began to sway.

"Eating with the servants," he croaked. "You never mentioned how ignorant she is of social customs, Rebbetzin." Mr. Grossfleisch looked squarely at Luska with his popping eyes. "Refined people do not eat with the servants."

"Why not? They do all the chores and cook the food, why shouldn't they sit at the table with us?"

"Well, well, what a little rabble-rouser we have here."

The Rabbi waved his hand. "Mr. Grossfleisch, she is an innocent child."

Luska did not like this man. He looked like a giant bullfrog with his bug eyes, broad nose and thick neck, and he sounded like one, too.

"But your children are certainly well behaved," Mr. Grossfleisch added. "And what a fine son you have, Rabbi, a bright and considerate young man. I am pleased he is the same age as our Ruthie."

His wife slipped her arm through her husband's. "So this is the poor little orphan you are trying to sponsor, Rebbetzin." Mrs. Grossfleisch's sharp voice made Luska shudder. "I have never seen a poverty ravaged child up close."

She peered down her nose at Luska, studying her like

she was deciding on a chicken to slaughter. "How thin she is, no meat on her bones. Look, Eben, she cannot fill out Ruthie's dress."

"Who is Ruthie?" Luska wondered aloud.

Mrs. Grossfleisch had the same mean smile as Saul. "Ruthie is our daughter. You are wearing one of the dresses she outgrew."

"Mrs. Grossfleisch was 'kind' enough to put those dresses in the poor box. That is where I found them for you," Saul taunted.

Mrs. Grossfleisch patted the boy's shoulder. "When we donated such fine clothing we expected it would go to some deserving girl."

Luska looked down at the dress she never wanted, the dress she wore only to please Saul. Saul! She thought he had become her friend, but he tricked her into misbehaving. Worse, she went against everything her parents taught her, and for what?

She tore open the buttons, yanked the dress over her head, and threw it before Mrs. Grossfleisch's feet. Standing before everyone stripped to her shtetl undergarments, she cried, "Then put it back in the poor box for someone else who needs it. I'll only wear my own dresses from now on!"

Mr. Grossfleisch nudged the Rabbi and chuckled. "Why look at her. Well dressed, impeccable manners, gracious and cultured; I can see why you are so taken with her."

The Rabbi stiffened. "The child comes from a poor village. She is unfamiliar with our way of life." He patted Luska's shoulder. "Lala, would you please go upstairs now? We shall talk about this later." He turned to his guests. "I must apologize about this again, Mr. and Mrs. Grossfleisch."

Luska didn't care that the meal was over, for her heart ached and her stomach churned too much to think about food. She ran from the table to her room. There on the bed, next to her precious bundle, was the other dress Saul had taken from the poor box. Luska flung it into the hallway and slammed the door behind her.

She fumed over how the Zedeks had betrayed her, until she remembered that she embarrassed them in front of important guests. They would be angry, too—with her.

"...when I mentioned we were considering adopting her, not one could fathom why we would endeavor to save this child ..."

Did she ruin everything? She crushed her bundle against her, tears streaming down her face.

She heard footsteps halt outside her room. Panicked, she curled up on the floor between the bed and the night table, her face buried in her bundle to cover the sound of her weeping. Whoever it was walked away. She tiptoed to the door and peeked out. The dress was gone, replaced by a tray with food. She left it there and returned to her hiding spot.

"Mama, Papa, why did you bring me here and then leave me all alone," she sobbed, looking to the ceiling. "Please come back and help me. Please!"

A rap at the door sent a bolt of fear through her.

"Lala, may we come in?" the Rabbi called through the door.

Luska held her breath. Please don't send me away, she begged silently. She tucked her bundle under her arm and opened the door.

The Rabbi came into the room with his hands clasped before him. His blank expression gave her no clue as to what he wanted. Luska trembled when the Rebbetzin entered and took a seat in the big chair, looking sad despite her pleasant smile. She then turned to the Rabbi.

"I am truly sorry about what happened tonight," he acknowledged calmly.

Luska was about to explain when he raised his hand. "Please let me finish before you say anything."

She tensed, prepared for the worst.

He began to pace, taking measured steps between the

door and the edge of the bed. "I should never have agreed to let you children dine alone. I should have insisted that you eat with us in the dining room, no matter what the Grossfleischs think. You have been through so much, more than I can imagine. It never occurred to me that you would not be able to handle something like this."

Luska eyed him cautiously as he stopped in front of her.

"You are such a brave little girl, Lala, and now I realize you are spirited, too." He issued a little smile at that. "I made a promise to you last night to help you. Instead I left you on your own, without guidance, and for that I am truly sorry."

The Rebbetzin beckoned her over. "You have every right to be angry, but please, do not be angry with me...or my family." She extended her arms, offering a hug.

Luska wasn't sure what to do, but she needed a friend in this house as much as she needed comforting. She moved closer until the Rebbetzin's warm arms wrapped around her, and she fell into a soothing embrace.

The Rebbetzin wasn't Mama, and would never be. But this woman was all she had, and at this moment, that was enough.

Chapter Fifteen

Horrible images invaded Luska's sleep and she awoke with a start, chomping on her lip to keep from crying out. She wiped the blood from her mouth and hugged her ball of laundry until she calmed down.

A slit of brightness between the draperies drew her to the window. Although the moon had already set on the far side of the house, its silver light gave the white flower patch in the yard a ghostly appearance. Thin shadows reached toward the fence. Sunrise would arrive soon. She saw a faint glow from two floors below and wondered if it came from Anya's room, if she couldn't sleep, either.

"You have been through so much, more than I can imagine..."

Her thoughts returned to her shtetl. It had only been a few days since the pogrom, yet somehow it seemed so long ago. She wanted more than anything to be back there again, but her home was gone. Having shelter and a meal wasn't enough, either. The Rabbi said she needed a home, with parents to guide her like Mama and Papa, but they were gone, too. She pressed her belongings to her chest and closed her eyes. The memory of the Rebbetzin's hug surrounded her in warmth; the scent of her, of powder and flowers, brought comfort, and for a moment, the pain that filled her heart was eased.

"Hershel, I want to keep her."

She couldn't have her old life back, but she could have a new one.

"I want that, too, Rebbetzin," she murmured to herself.

There it was. For the first time, she admitted it. She

wanted to stay here with the Zedeks and be their daughter. The Rebbetzin said she wanted to keep her, that she deserved to stay here. No more wandering, no more wondering. Somehow, she had to find a way to make that happen. Even if the Rabbi had misgivings. Even if it made Saul angry. Even if she had to stop thinking about Mama and Papa to please the Zedeks.

The thought made her cringe, but if it had to be....

Luska stared out through the window until darkness melted into day.

The Rabbi and his children were finishing their breakfast when Luska joined them. With no newspaper to hide behind, the Rabbi looked stern this morning. Saul appeared grumpy, but Esther seemed her charming self.

"Good morning," Luska mumbled before sitting down.

"Good morning, Lala" the Rabbi said without feeling.

"G' mornee" chirped Esther. "Where you pretty dress?"

"She threw them away," growled Saul.

Luska buried her face in her hands. She didn't think about how her show of defiance last night would insult Saul. A tug on her foot opened her eyes. Esther had pulled off one of her shoes.

"Now you Ash Girl. Prince come."

The Rabbi tapped the table. "Esther, give Lala back her shoe. There will be no princes coming to this house."

Anya set a plate and a glass of milk on the table for Luska. The maid had dark circles under her eyes.

"Anya, where is my wife?" The Rabbi sounded impatient.

Anya served Luska a big portion of bread and cheese. "I'm sorry, Rabbi, she won't be coming down for breakfast.

102

Madam is feeling...unwell."

Saul tugged on the Rabbi's sleeve. "Father, I do not feel well, either."

The Rabbi felt the boy's forehead. He asked Anya, "Is it serious? Should I have Vostok fetch the doctor?"

Anya smiled. "No, Rabbi, but I expect this will continue...for a few months."

"Oh?" At first he seemed puzzled, but then he smiled. "Ohhhh."

"I think I have what Mother has," Saul moaned as his father withdrew his palm.

"No, Saul, I can say with complete assurance you do not."

"Rabbi, being as Madam is indisposed, at what time would you like the children to be ready for Sabbath services?" Anya gave Luska a wink.

"We must leave in half an hour." He got up and dropped his napkin on his chair. "I trust there will be enough time."

"I'll have all three dressed and ready by then."

"That will not be necessary. Please see to my children. Lala will stay here."

Anya looked as disappointed as Luska felt.

"But Rabbi, why can't I go, too? Am I being punished for last night?"

"Not at all, Lala. The Rebbetzin believes there is much you need to learn about proper behavior before you go to our synagogue, and I must agree. We want you to...fit in."

Fit in. Not proper. Yesterday the Rebbetzin said her clothes weren't right. Today her behavior wasn't right. No matter how hard she tried, nothing she said, nothing she did ever seemed to be right.

Finding a way to stay would be harder than she thought.

Chapter Sixteen

Luska slumped on her bed. She could hear the excitement of the children down the hall as they prepared to meet their father. The three of them would soon walk to the synagogue, like she used to do every Saturday with Mama and Papa.

She always looked forward to the Sabbath. Right before sundown on Friday, Papa would pour a thimble of schnapps to drink after Mama lit the candles. She had the table set for supper with her heirloom cloth, ready for whatever she had prepared, maybe potato dumplings, or chicken if they had one to slaughter. On Saturday, they would often visit with other families in the village. They might walk in the meadow if the weather was pleasant, but in winter the three of them would huddle near the stove while Papa entertained them with stories about his peddling trips. At sundown, she and Mama would check the tablecloth to see if it needed laundering or if it could be put it away for next week.

Tears threatened. She pulled Papa's shirt from her laundry and wrapped it around her, but it didn't help. Things here might be fancier, but they could never replace what was forever lost.

"No more wishing for the past," she sighed as she returned the shirt to her bundle.

She must try to forget about the life she knew if she had any hope of staying with the Zedeks.

Next week will be different, she thought as she fought back tears. Next week, I will go to the synagogue with them.

* * * * *

The Rebbetzin hadn't come out of her room yet. Luska felt useless with nothing to do, like that poor little girl with the empty eyes, and her feeling of emptiness worsened. Glancing around the room, looking for a chore, an activity, anything to distract her from her memories, she finally locked on the dresser with the rabbits painted on the knobs. One by one she peeked into each drawer, all empty except the one she opened yesterday, which held the blue velvet suit and white shirt. Whose clothes were these? She ran her fingertips across the plush fabric.

"Miss, may I come in?" Anya called through the door.

Luska shut the drawer. "Yes, please."

Anya entered with her hands behind her. "I'm sorry about what happened. If I hadn't left you alone last night, well, I can't help but feel it was my fault."

"No, I'm to blame. I knew better than to act that foolishly, but Saul made me so angry I did it anyway." Luska grimaced. "I should have known he didn't really like me."

"I know you did your best. Everyone realizes that now." Anya gave her a sympathetic grin. "I have a little surprise to cheer you up."

She held up a yellow dress with a blue floral apron trimmed in lace. It had a crisp white collar with matching cuffs. "What do you think of this?"

"Oh my," gasped Luska. "It's the most beautiful dress I've ever seen. Whose is it?"

Anya's smile broadened. "It's yours."

"Mine?" She reached out and touched the soft fabric. "But how could that be?"

"I made it for you." Anya unbuttoned the back.

Luska hesitated. "For me? Why?"

"It's my way of saying, 'sorry,' for last night. A gift for your Sabbath. I'd hoped you could wear it to the synagogue, but at least you can wear it here. Would you like to try it on?"

"Oh yes, please." After undressing, Luska slipped it on

and Anya tied the lace-trimmed belt into a bow in back. Together they walked to the toilette so Luska could see herself in the mirror. The dress looked even prettier on and fit her perfectly.

She threw her arms around Anya. "No one has ever done anything like this for me before. How can I ever thank you?"

"You just did, Miss," she beamed.

Luska turned back and forth before the mirror. "I want everyone to see me in this."

"Why don't you show it to Madam? She's awake now. Seeing you dressed up is sure to cheer her spirits."

When the Rebbetzin invited her into the bedroom, Luska instead posed in the doorway.

The Rebbetzin sat up in bed, looking very happy.

"Oh, my, wherever did you get such a lovely dress?"

Luska turned in a circle. "Miss Anya made it for me." She scampered over to the bed, one of two in the large room. The dark wood furniture, simple in form and decoration, lacked the curved lines and golden trim of the pieces downstairs.

The Rebbetzin lifted the skirt and ran her hand over the material. "She must have taken part of one dress and added it to the other, though I cannot tell what she used for the collar and cuffs. What a fine job. It must have taken hours."

"I think she stayed up all night."

"Really? I must talk to her. There might be enough fabric left over from that piglet's clothing to recover a chair."

"What's a piglet?"

"A very impolite comment about the Grossfleischs' daughter, so please forget I said it. It shall stay between us?" She patted the mattress.

Luska hopped up on the bed. "I promise I won't tell." She decided "piglet" meant the Grossfleischs' daughter was as horrible as her parents. The thought pleased her as much as being trusted with the secret.

The Rebbetzin rubbed the hem of Luska's dress between her thumb and forefinger. "Anya must be very fond of you."

"I like Miss Anya. She's been very kind to me."

"She is kind. The poor woman has so little, and yet she is still good natured and generous, while others, who have everything a person could want, can be cold and uncaring, even cruel." She stared off into the distance. "I never believed that people who had so little could truly be happy in life, but perhaps I have been mistaken about that."

Luska didn't understand what the Rebbetzin meant, so she said nothing.

A warm breeze fluttered the lace curtains in the window. The Rebbetzin's attention remained there. Luska used those quiet moments to consider how she could overcome the Rabbi's concerns...

She looked around the room. "Where is the Rebbetzin?"

He exhaled. "Your nightmare scared the children. I hope she's with them."

"Rebbetzin, I'm sorry I woke everyone the other night when I screamed. I keep having scary dreams, but I promise to be quiet from now on."

She patted Luska on the leg. "You have nothing to apologize for, child. You lived through something dreadful, absolutely dreadful."

"But I don't want to bother your family. Then they won't like me, and they'll want to send me away."

The woman's face tightened. "I will not allow that. I have plans for you."

"Hershel, I want to keep her."

Luska smiled and sat a little closer to the Rebbetzin. The woman smiled back at her and then turned away.

"Anya told me you offered to do some housework, like

making your bed."

"I didn't know she and Mr. Vostok did all of the chores. I thought I had to help. I always did chores at home."

"I see." The Rebbetzin turned back and stared at Luska for a long while without saying anything. It made Luska nervous, and she looked down until the woman spoke again.

"Tell me, dear, do you enjoy doing chores?"

Luska didn't understand. "They have to be done, so I do them. When Papa—"

"But would you rather not do them?" the Rebbetzin interrupted.

"No, I want to do chores. The women in the shtetl always said that if you have nothing to do, it means you have nothing. Only young ones don't do chores and I'm not a little girl anymore, I'm almost eight."

"You really are not a child anymore, are you?" Now the Rebbetzin looked down. "Were there any chores you liked better—that is, if you had a choice between cleaning the bedroom, washing clothes, or helping in the kitchen, which would you rather do?"

"I always did what I could, I never thought..." Luska brightened. "Is that what you want, Rebbetzin? Because I would be happy to do chores for you, whatever you wanted, and I'd do a good job, too. Mama always said—"

"That is good to know. I am thankful you feel that way about doing house...doing chores, that is. Tonight, after the Sabbath, the Rabbi and I will talk more about this with you." She gave Luska's hand a reassuring pat. "It must be close to lunchtime. I had Anya prepare a tray for you before she left for the afternoon. You should go downstairs and eat."

"Won't you come with me?"

The Rebbetzin lay down, waving her hand. "No, dear, I could not stand the sight of food right now, let alone the smell. You go, though."

"Eat alone?"

"Perhaps Vostok can keep you company. In fact, why not have your lunch in the kitchen? You made a good point last night, when you said you wanted to eat with the servants. Tell him I said you should."

Luska slid off the bed. She heard the Rebbetzin moan as she settled into her pillows.

"You look very pretty in that, child, but you should keep your old dresses for now."

"I will." Luska spread out her skirt. "I want to save this for special days, like the Sabbath."

"That is very sensible."

Luska left the Rebbetzin's room even more pleased than when she entered. She had hoped to find a way to stay with the Zedeks and now she had a real chance. The Rebbetzin wanted her do chores, like she did at home for Mama and Papa. The Zedeks would be so proud of her. Maybe when they saw how well Luska did them, Saul and Esther would be given chores, too.

At last she began to feel like part of the family. She'd do her chores and the servants would do the housework. Although she wasn't sure how chores differed from housework, she decided they must.

Doing chores for the Zedeks would be a good thing – it would, wouldn't it?

Chapter Seventeen

A tray of rolls and a dish of currant preserves awaited Luska on the table in the breakfast room. Shadows darkened the corridor leading to the stairway and the floor below.

"...why not have your lunch in the kitchen...you wanted to eat with the servants...."

"...Vostok and I don't eat with the family or their guests."

She walked to the edge of the stairs and peered down. Vostok would be there. She could show him how proper she looked.

"More than proper, Miss, you look lovely."

That's what I'll do, she thought, I'll go downstairs to see...what he thinks of my dress.

As Luska descended, uneasiness gripped her with each step and she almost turned back, but her curiosity outweighed her discomfort. At the bottom was a long, narrow hallway with rooms ahead and behind.

She peered into the first room, a spotless kitchen with wood cabinets, a large stove, two metal sinks, and a plankwood table with two chairs anchored in the center. She nodded; so that's where they eat. Next to the kitchen was a storage room, with sacks and crates stacked along the side walls, and a servant's entrance in back. She continued her exploration on the other side of the stairway.

She scarcely believed this was part of the Zedek house, with its dim hallway, low ceilings and cramped rooms. The downstairs quarters looked dull without the beautiful furnishings that filled the rooms above. Even though her home had been much smaller, she felt closed in down here. It set her nerves on edge.

Luska glanced into a tiny bedroom with a blue spread on the bed and a rag rug on the floor. A discolored table and chair sat between a pair of tiny windows tucked under the ceiling, one hung with blue flowered curtains and the other one bare. Anya's sewing basket rested in the chair. The bodice of a child's dress, made from the curtain fabric, lay over the chair back.

A floorboard creaked behind her. She pressed her back against the wall and peeked through the open door into the room across the hall. Inside sat Vostok, reading a book. The room looked much like Anya's except for a small shelf holding some books and, next to the door, a tall pole with pegs. His formal black jacket hung on one side, and on the other, his apron, which looked a lot shorter than it did yesterday.

"I don't know what she used for the collars and cuffs...."

Now, Luska knew.

Vostok's window faced the street, and through it Luska could see the feet of two people climbing the steps to the front door. Vostok must have noticed their footsteps, too, for he rose to put on his jacket. Luska ducked into Anya's room before he could see her as he headed to the stairway. She trailed upstairs behind him and hid off to the side as he opened the door.

On the landing stood a short man and a much shorter woman. Vostok looked surprised when he saw them.

"Good afternoon, sir, madam."

"Hello, Vostok, it's nice to see you again. How are you?" the woman asked.

Now Vostok looked uncomfortable.

"Very well, thank you, madam." He paused. "I heard that your mother passed on recently. My condolences. She was a fine, gracious woman."

"Thank you." The woman choked up, and so did Luska.

The man removed his hat. "We are here to see Naomi."

112

"I'm not sure if she's up to visitors, sir. She's been feeling unwell today."

"Would you please check with her? We have some important news."

"Yes," added the woman, "very good news."

Vostok almost smiled. "How wonderful."

The woman shook her head. "No, not that, unfortunately. Almost as good, though."

Luska noticed the woman had wavy black hair, much like Mama's.

"I will announce you to Madam." Vostok cleared his throat. "I'm terribly sorry, but you will have to wait here."

The man looked disappointed, but nodded. The woman scowled.

"Do what you must," she fumed. "We don't want to put you in the middle of this."

Luska hid until Vostok was out of sight. She observed the couple waiting at the door; nicely dressed, though their clothes lacked the elegant tailoring favored by the Rabbi and his wife. The man stood with his hands clasped behind his back. He had the same blue eyes as the Rebbetzin, and the same light brown hair, only less of it. And although she understood what they said, the words sounded different when they spoke.

"Do you think she'll see us?" The woman asked him.

The man shrugged. "She might, if she feels well enough."

"I wouldn't wager on it." She turned to him. "Look at you, your tie's all crooked." She reached up to straighten his tie and brush lint from his jacket, which dislodged a small tan chip. Luska watched it float to the ground. The man smiled at the woman while she fussed over him.

"Try not to make me look too handsome," he joked, and the woman rolled her eyes. They landed on Luska.

"Why, hello there. Who are you," the woman asked.

"I'm called Lala." She curtsied.

"What a pretty girl you are. Are you a friend of Saul?"

"Oh no!" she cried. "I could never be his friend."

The woman chuckled. "Pretty, and smart as well."

"Sarah, please," the man admonished. The woman did not apologize, nor did she look sorry for what she said.

Vostok returned, nodding to Luska as he approached the two visitors. "I'm very sorry, but Madam is...she's not feeling up to company today. Perhaps another time?"

The woman turned to her husband. "Didn't I tell you, Jakob? Let's go. Thank you, Vostok. It was a pleasure seeing you again."

"And you, Madam. Good day. Good day sir."

Vostok waited until the couple went down the steps before he turned to Luska.

"That wasn't so, what you said to those people, was it?"

Vostok raised an eyebrow. "What do you mean?"

"When you told them to come back another time, your face smiled, but your eyes didn't."

His stern look warned of a scolding. "May I ask what you're doing here, Miss?"

"I came to thank you."

"For what?"

She touched her collar. "For this."

His mouth curled into the hint of a smile. As the door closed, the chip that fell from the man's jacket was drawn into the house. Luska waited until Vostok went downstairs before picking it up. It was something she had found countless times in front of her house where Papa sat—a wood shaving. She slipped it in her pocket.

Instead of returning upstairs, she walked toward the hallway leading to the finely furnished rooms that so impressed her that first night. But when she opened the double doors to the sitting room, she felt like she was in a different place. Partly closed draperies shrouded the room in shadow. Too many things filled the room. Each piece looked beautiful by itself, but together they were like loud voices shouting over each other. Why did she still feel uncomfortable in here? Perhaps it's the darkness, she thought as she left the room. The sitting room lost much of its sparkle without the brilliant light of the ceiling lamps.

Luska closed the doors behind her. She stopped in the darkened hallway to gaze at the painting of the Rebbetzin. The warmth was gone from her eyes, the caring from her expression. Without light, the woman on the canvas looked flat and unreal.

She returned to the breakfast room, where the platter of food sat waiting for her. She reached for a roll but put it back. Her appetite disappeared, replaced by a sharp pang of loneliness. She ran upstairs to her room, pressed her bundle to her chest, and sat in a corner, rocking back and forth, until sunset drew its curtain of darkness over the house.

Chapter Eighteen

At sundown, the Zedeks ended the Sabbath with traditional prayers and a simple dinner of broth, potted meat, and potatoes. Everyone was dressed in different clothing than earlier. In the three days since Luska had been in their house, no one in the family had worn the same garment more than once.

Anya had dressed the dining room table with a plain white cloth and fewer pieces of silverware. A basket of pink flowers was the only decoration.

Luska sat alone at one long side of the table, her place set equally distant from the Rabbi and his wife. Her excitement over the Rebbetzin's plans had faded, replaced with bad visions that overwhelmed her. The harder she tried to forget her past, the stronger it came back to haunt her.

The children talked about their day in a most carefree manner. Hearing them brought on sadness. Her place within the family remained uncertain. Every story, every giggle, made her decision seem that much harder, her goal that much farther away. She had to find a way to overcome this constant melancholy, but right now she could not bring herself to do so. She kept her head down while she picked at her food, preferring to avoid Saul's glares, or worse, the Rebbetzin's inattention. Even little Esther ignored her.

"I am very hungry tonight." The Rabbi beckoned to Anya and she brought the half empty serving platter to him. "It was a busy day. I talked to the Grossfleischs...."

Luska put her fork down. Her appetite disappeared at the mention of their name.

"They enjoyed having dinner with us last night," he continued.

"I spent most of the day with them, Mother," Saul piped in.

The Rabbi helped himself to another potato. "He did. They are very fond of you, Saul."

The Rebbetzin dropped her napkin onto her half finished plate of food. "Shall I invite them again in a few weeks?" Her voice sounded weary.

"I can ask them tomorrow. We have a meeting scheduled in my office in the morning."

The Rebbetzin became happy. "I have an appointment tomorrow morning as well."

The Rabbi locked eyes with his wife and they both smiled.

Luska pressed back into her chair and sipped water while the children talked about their day. She felt as far away from the family as she did from the table.

Anya waited to the side with a tray to clear the dishes. The Rabbi rose from his chair and gestured to her to put the tray down.

"Anya, the table can wait. Would you put the children to bed tonight?"

Saul pouted. "But I want Mother to tuck me in," he sniveled. "I have not seen her all day." His head dropped to his chest. The Rabbi gave the boy's head a quick pat.

"I am sorry, son. Your mother will tuck you in tomorrow night."

He gave his wife a smile, but his eyes were pleading.

"Yes...tomorrow," she finally said.

"Tonight your mother and I must speak with Lala about an important matter. Lala, would you join us in the sitting room?"

The lamps had been lit before they entered, returning the room to its golden glory, but a feeling of dread rattled Luska as she entered. Was it memories of its shadowy appearance earlier in the day, or what might be said tonight

118

that caused the tumbling in her stomach? She bit her lip as she stared at the rug. One side of its border of flowers lay hidden under the furniture.

The Rabbi offered her a seat across from the Rebbetzin. He poured a brown liquid from a crystal bottle and offered it to his wife, which she declined with a wave of her hand. He cradled the glass in his palm as he stepped back and forth across the exposed border of the rug.

"Lala, my wife and I have been discussing your situation. She has an idea that she feels may be helpful." He took a sip of his drink. "She would like Anya to show you how to do some housekeeping—"

"Chores, dear," the Rebbetzin interjected. "She calls them chores."

"Then how to do some chores around the house." The Rabbi tugged at his collar and took another sip from his glass. Luska turned to the Rebbetzin, who kept her eyes on her husband. He stopped pacing. The carpet flowers lay crushed beneath his feet.

"What about Miss Anya and Mr. Vostok? What will they do?" Luska asked.

"They will still have their place here," the Rebbetzin assured her with a small smile. "It is just that I am...I will need more help around the house, so since you told me you did not mind doing chores... I thought that for as long as you stay here...."

"...stay here...

Luska lit up at those words. "Oh, yes, Rebbetzin, yes, I would be so happy to do chores for you as long as I can stay here."

The Rabbi waved his hand. "Please understand, Lala, I am not convinced that this is a good plan. I would still prefer to find a family to adopt you as I promised."

"Yes, dear, but you also promised me that if she agrees to train with Anya, you would allow it."

He nodded. "My wife feels that if you learn how to keep house, it would create more opportunities to place you."

"And in the meantime, you will stay here and work on your chores," his wife added. "And if you learn quickly…" she looked at her husband again. "Then we shall see." The Rebbetzin turned back to Luska. "But you must be willing to work hard and learn the proper way to do these chores. Will you?"

The trampled flowers had survived the Rabbi's steps and plumped back to their full beauty. How many times had they been flattened, only to rise up again like wildflowers after the spring thaw? An old saying from her village rang in her ears—each dawn brings a promise new.

"When shall I start?"

Chapter Nineteen

Luska awoke in the middle of the night. Clinging to the wall, she tiptoed down the dark hallway to the toilette, worried that every floorboard that squeaked beneath her steps might wake the family. She heard more creaking while inside and reminded herself that the house often made noises at night. Afterwards, she crept back to her room as quietly as possible and tumbled into bed.

Something was wrong. She wasn't sure what it was until she reached out and felt...nothing. She ran her hands around the mattress, but there wasn't anything tangled in the blankets or resting on the pillow. Her bundle was gone!

Luska leapt out of bed, heart thumping wildly, head pounding. Panic gripped her so fiercely she clamped her teeth together to keep from crying out and scaring everyone. Her precious bundle – she had to find it.

She ran to the windows and flung open the draperies. The light of the full moon streamed into the room. Luska searched the floor, first with her eyes and then on her hands and knees. She looked under the bed, around the little table and chair, behind the dresser, and beneath the skirt of the big chair.

"Oh, no, where could it be," she whispered to herself. "Did I bring it to the toilette and leave it there? I don't think I did, but maybe....?"

Once again she padded down the hallway. She checked the toilette with care, but as she suspected, it wasn't in there. She was too upset to worry about the house creaking again.

Luska's breathing became panting, which made her

dizzy. She sat down and tried to catch her breath, tried to think. What could have happened to it?

"I do not like you and I do not want you here."

Saul.

No one else would have taken it but him. Saul hated her. He did everything he could to drive her away from his parents and out of their home. She remembered his frightening visit to her room that first night in the house.

Now it was her turn to visit.

She opened his bedroom door slowly to drag out the creaky sound it made, hoping he'd give himself away. He lay in bed, motionless, but Luska believed deep in her heart he was pretending to be asleep, that the noises she heard while in the toilette were made by him sneaking through the hall and into her room.

Saul kept still. She began searching under his bed, around the floor, and behind the dresser, but she didn't find her bundle. A loud snort from the master bedroom startled her; the Rabbi was snoring. She waited for him to stop and then turned her attention to the boy in the bed.

She watched Saul as the house fell silent again. He didn't move, but his breathing became more rapid the longer she stood there. Finally, she said in her darkest voice, "I know you're awake."

He popped up in bed like Esther's Jack-in-the-Box. "What are you doing in my room? I did not say you could come in."

"And I never said you could take my things, but you did."

"I have no idea what you mean," he sniffed.

"I know you snuck in and stole my bundle when I left the room. I heard the creaking in the hallway when you did it. Give it back to me, now." She blinked back tears. "It's all I have in the world."

"Now why would I take your rag bag?"

122

"Because you hate me, that's why," she growled through clenched teeth.

His mouth flew open in horror. "Oh, no! I never said I hate you. Never, never, never!" His voice grew loud and even in the dark she could see his panic.

"Shhhh," she implored. "You'll wake your parents."

"Then do not say that, ever!"

"Why not? You're mean to me, you've tricked me, and you said you wished I would die, too. What else would I think?"

He wilted before her. "I want you to go away, so I can have my Mother back."

"But Saul, I'm not taking your mother away."

"Yes, you are. She spends more time with you than with me. I have always had to share her, first with David, then Esther, and now you, too."

"Who's David?"

"He was my brother. He had a terrible sickness before he died. We are not allowed to talk about him, ever." Saul checked the door before continuing. "The servants were afraid of him; they thought he was a monster, 'A bedeviled creature' they called him. Father said there is no such thing as devils, but everyone left us because of him." His voice dropped even lower. "They all feared he was possessed by the devil, with those red spots in his eyes and unholy shaking and foaming at the mouth. But Mother loved him, more than anyone else in the world, so she made them all go away because they hated him." He caught his breath. "I hated him, too, but I could never say so."

And with that, Saul instantly changed from a nasty brat to a sad little boy. Luska's heart softened and she hugged him. He allowed it. Another window of hope opened before her.

"That's why you were so upset when I said you hated me. You were afraid your mother would send you away, too."

He nodded. "David was finally gone and I had Mother back, and then you show up, with the same brown hair and dark eyes. And what does Mother do? She puts you in his room, with all of his things, and in his bed." His voice grew cold again. "I heard her tell Father she wanted to keep you."

Did he know of his mother's plans to have her stay?

"But that's only if they can't find a family to take me in. Otherwise I would be sent away to an orphanage and your parents said that would be a sin."

"Nobody else wants you."

His words hurt like a slap. Her eyes filled with bitter tears that stung as much as the truth.

"Mother wants you, though. You want that, too."

"It's true, I do want to stay, but I don't want to take your mother and father away from you. I just don't want to be sent away. I need a home and a family, Saul. Can't I share yours?"

His glum face turned sour again. "No. Esther is bad enough. I do not want you here."

He wouldn't change his mind and knowing why made it impossible to fight him. Perhaps she could still win one battle.

"All I have left in the world is my, my ball of rags. Please give it back to me."

He shrugged. "Did you look under your bed?"

"Of course, it was the first place...." She remembered hearing the floor creak while she searched the toilette.

Luska hurried back to her room and dropped to the floor by the bed. There it was. Seizing the bundle as though it were life itself, she buried her face in it. Relief flowed through her body, followed by exhaustion.

She kept the draperies slightly open before crawling under the blanket, her precious ball cradled in her arms, but she couldn't fall asleep. The night's experience played over and over in her mind. Saul wished she would leave. The Rabbi intended to send her somewhere else. Only the Rebbetzin wanted her to stay and help out by doing chores. Mama and Papa sometimes disagreed, but after a time one of them would always give in. Who would win the argument about her...the Rabbi, or his wife?

"I heard her tell Father she wanted to keep you."

"You will stay with us...."

"I do not want you here."

"I still hope to find a family to adopt you...."

"Nobody else wants you."

Everything was so mixed up.

Moonlight fell between the parted draperies and pooled on top of the chest that held David's clothes. She ran her finger along the stem of her tulip, which yesterday stood tall. It now curved over the lip of the vase, its golden petals facing downward as if it were sad, too

Her mind spun – stay, go, chores...David.

"David was my brother".

Saul called him a monster.

"But Mother loved him, more than anyone else in the world."

Chapter Twenty

Anya carried the breakfast dishes downstairs as the Rabbi, his children, and Luska left the room. The Rebbetzin met them outside and motioned to Luska to wait with her until the others went upstairs. She handed Luska a half apron.

"Go to the sitting room and wait for Anya."

Luska tied the apron over her gray dress. "Yes, Rebbetzin."

A few minutes passed before Anya entered the room carrying a tall crystal vase filled with flowers from the backyard. She must not have seen Luska for she went directly to the high chest without saying hello. Anya dried the bottom of the vase with a rag from her cleaning basket and then reached up to dust the top of the chest before placing the vase there. She took a fresh rag to wipe the flat front of the chest with long strokes, followed by short, quick movements across the heavily carved panels which bordered the top.

"Good morning, Miss Anya."

She turned with a start. "Oh, hello Miss, what are you doing...may I ask why you're dressed like that?"

"The Rabbi asked me to do some chores. There's so much to do in this house and the Rebbetzin wanted me to help, so she said you would show me what to do, and how to do it, and...Miss Anya, are you crying?"

Anya pressed the corner of her apron to her eyes. She began to say something but all that came out was a choked back sob.

"Please don't cry. The Rabbi promised me that you and Mr. Vostok would still work here. You've been so kind to me. I would never do anything to hurt you." Luska waved her arm. "This is a big house. There must be plenty of work for all of us," she grinned. "And if I do a good job, the Rebbetzin said I could stay. Wouldn't that be wonderful?" She got no response.

"Excuse me, but I must speak to Madam about this." Anya marched out of the sitting room.

Luska assumed the Rebbetzin hadn't told Anya about their plans, and Anya would not take the word of a child like herself.

While waiting for the maid to return, Luska studied the flower-filled vase atop the chest. It looked so beautiful when Anya brought it in, but its beauty was lost on its high perch. There was something wrong about the chest there, which the sitting room lights last night had not changed, nor did the pretty white flowers. She shook her head. That vase would look better somewhere else, someplace lower.

Anya returned to the sitting room, her face blank. Silently, she lifted her cleaning basket and handed a few rags to Luska.

"I have been instructed to teach you the finer points of housekeeping." Her voice sounded dull. "We'll begin today with dusting." Anya looked around the room. "You're too short to reach most of the top surfaces, but those little fingers are perfect for the ornate decorations." She pointed to a small table with bands of gold-colored carving along its legs. "Step over to this console and I'll show you how it's done."

"I know how, Miss Anya, I watched you do it." Luska ran the dust rag over every centimeter of one leg and then the others, using the same method Anya had used. When she was done, Anya nodded, but without enthusiasm. Her reaction disappointed Luska, who wanted her work to please Anya as much as the Rebbetzin. She would have to try harder.

The Rebbetzin peeked into the room and smiled. "How is she progressing?"

"Fine, Madam."

"What will you have her do?"

"I thought she could clean the carved pieces."

Luska held up her hands. "Little fingers." She wiggled them.

"Perfect. Oh, and the objet d'art. Have her clean the small pieces as well."

"But they're so fragile, Madam. What if something breaks?"

The Rebbetzin addressed Luska. "You will be very careful, yes?"

Luska returned her smile. "I will, Rebbetzin, I'll do a very good job. You'll see."

"I know you will. Then I shall leave you to it."

Anya and Luska continued their work without much conversation; Luska asked a few questions for which Anya gave brief but clear answers. Luska decided she didn't mind dusting; it allowed her to touch the furniture and see their decoration up close. She began with the four matching chairs facing the settee. She ran her rag down the dark wood legs until she found a surprise at the bottom.

"Ooh, look at this, Miss Anya. The chairs have bird's feet and they're holding a ball," she exclaimed. "Even the talons look real."

"They do, don't they." Anya grew serious again. "There's much to do. Please continue with your cleaning."

Anya removed a blizzard of figurines atop two matching cabinets. It exposed their gleaming black tops, streaked with white and sparkly bits. When Luska pressed her hand on the surface, it felt cool.

"What is this made of?"

Anya glanced over her shoulder. "It's marble. Dust it the same way as wood."

As Luska ran her rag across one cabinet door, it opened to reveal a pair of tall containers, in sky blue and white, dotted with raised pink flowers. She stared, enchanted by their perfect shape, and wondered why anyone would hide away such wonderful pieces. Despite the number of similar items scattered throughout the sitting room, few looked as beautiful as these.

Anya came to check on her. "I don't know why Madam keeps those ewers in there. She must have forgotten about them with all the things in this room."

Luska discovered more wonderful secrets as her rag-covered fingers traced the raised mounds and carved hollows of the furniture. A treasure trove of vases and bowls, boxes and statues lay hidden behind cabinet doors or crammed on lower shelves, out of sight.

She worked on a small chest with a slanted front. Although it didn't have the elaborate gilt and carving of the other pieces of furniture; she liked its simple beauty the best. The front panels were filled with different bits of wood, patched together like a quilt, and the legs looked like candles covered with rows of dripped wax, which tapered to a cuff of gold lace. She dusted a footed bowl of creamy stone perched on top; a gold garland encircled its wide oval rim. Luska peered closer at what she thought were handles. They were, instead, odd looking babies seated on each side of the bowl, holding the garland. She thought the bowl looked too big for that exquisite chest.

Once they finished dusting, Anya gathered all the room's statues, bowls and figurines on the settee.

"Next, you can work on the art objects. The ones with a shiny glaze are porcelain and the dull surfaced pieces are bisque, but they're cleaned the same way." She lifted a bowl and wiped it thoroughly while Luska watched. "See how it's done...Lala? Now you try it."

Luska reviewed the array of pieces cluttering the cushions. It took both hands for her to lift a porcelain figure of a cat-like creature with dark spots on its tan body. She liked how it was posed—head lifted high, mouth open, its front paws clinging to a rock, and its back legs coiled.

"What is this?" It reminded her of a Bible story. "Is it a lion?"

"I don't know. Some kind of jungle animal, I suppose."

"It looks so wild, standing on the rock, like it's ready to leap."

The maid sighed. "There's a lot to do today, Lala, so we should get back to work." She picked up her cleaning basket. "I must start working in the dining room now. Come fetch me when you're done and I'll show you where everything goes."

"I will." Luska glanced back at the settee. "I'm going to like cleaning all of these wonderful things." She meant that, so why did Anya look back at her so sorrowfully?

The woman tenderly cupped Luska's chin in her hand and tried to look pleased, but she couldn't even manage a smile. Instead she lowered her head and dashed from the room, pressing her apron to her face.

"Thank you for teaching me how to clean, Miss Anya." Luska called after her, hoping it would ease whatever was bothering her.

"See how it's done...Lala..."

Miss Anya had called her Lala today for the first time, instead of Miss.

"It wouldn't be right to call a guest by name, Miss."

It was clear to Luska she was no longer a guest, but she wasn't a member of the family, either, not yet. It would take more than a few chores to earn her that right – she had to do something special to set herself apart from the servants.

The final piece, a porcelain figurine of a girl holding a little white dog, sparkled like crystal now, but Luska liked it so much she didn't want to set it on the rug with the other pieces she had finished polishing, so she rubbed its invisible spots a little longer. When everything had been cleaned, she was supposed to fetch Anya to help put away the art objects, but instead, she put a few pieces on a bare table and moved them around, arranging things together in a manner that looked pleasing to her. The blue and white ewers she'd set on the pair of marble topped cabinets flattered each other. When most everything else was grouped together, she placed each group on a table or shelf. Then she tucked away the leftover items until the right place could be found for them. Lastly she rearranged some of the side chairs until they looked more comfortable in the room.

Once she was done she reviewed her work. That tall chest in the corner looked even worse after her changes, especially with that vase on top. If only she could reach it....

"What are you doing?"

Luska spun around to face Saul standing in the doorway. She froze. "I'm doing chores. Your mother asked me to."

Saul rubbed his hands together. "Good, that means you will have to live..." he stepped into the sitting room and looked around, his mouth agape. "What did you do to the room?" The boy sounded more curious than angry. "You moved things around."

"A little," Luska shrugged. "Everything except that vase. I wanted to move it to a lower table, but it's too high for me to reach."

"I shall help you move it," he volunteered.

Luska didn't respond, positive this must be some sort of trick.

He flashed a sly grin. "Do you want my help, or not?"

"I don't know." She frowned. "Why would you want to help me?"

He laughed. "Because when my Mother sees what you have done to her favorite room, she will never speak to you again." He sat on one of the bird feet chairs, still grinning.

Anger flared up in her, but the Rebbetzin's words came rushing back…

"….*you will stay with us*…."

They echoed louder and louder until they silenced the boy's prediction.

Luska relaxed and smiled back at Saul. She strode to the tall chest, her arms crossed. "Are you going to help me or not?"

They each took one end of a bird feet chair and carried it over to the tall chest. Saul steadied the chair back with both hands.

"I will hold it for you while you climb up."

She cast a doubtful eye at him.

"Go on, you foolish girl. Why would I do something that would get me into trouble?"

She stood on the chair, but couldn't quite reach the top of the chest.

"It's not high enough. What else can we use?"

"What about one of the tables?" Saul suggested.

Luska pointed to a side table. "That one looks tall enough."

"But it may not be strong enough to hold you. What about that one against the wall, with the heavy legs?"

She helped him carry the table next to the chest and clambered up. The vase was in easy reach. She lowered it to the table and climbed down. Together they returned the table to its place.

"Thank you for helping me, Saul. I can do the rest by myself. And I think your mother will like what I've done."

"And I think she will be so upset she will send you away." He laughed all the way out of the room.

Luska tied back the heavy draperies and closed the lace curtains underneath. Daylight filtered in, which cheered up the sitting room. Everything looked much better than before, but a scan of the room gave her one more idea. She removed most of the flowers from the crystal vase she'd brought down and divided the stems between the two ewers. The white petals brought out the blue in the vessels. She placed the vase on the table she had climbed on to bring it down.

With her chore completed, Luska went to get Anya. She led the maid to the sitting room doors, which she had shut to contain the surprise. After a moment's pause, Luska opened them to reveal her handiwork.

"Do you like what I did?"

Luska nearly panicked when Anya stood wide eyed in the doorway, just like Saul. Finally, Anya said, "It does look nice, but what will Madam say?"

"Let's ask her right now." A jubilant Luska seized Anya by the hand and dragged her along as she scurried down the hallway, up the stairs and straight to the master bedroom door, which opened before she could knock. The Rebbetzin emerged wearing a pale green dress with a short jacket and matching hat. She pulled on her summer gloves as she walked to the staircase.

"Are you going out, Rebbetzin?" Luska stood in front of her, blocking the way.

"Yes, I must leave right now." She placed her hand over her belly. "I have a very important appointment."

"Rebbetzin, please, before you go, could you come to the sitting room? I want to show you something."

"I do not have the time and I am sure you did a fine job...." She turned to Anya, but the maid wore a blank expression. "Oh, I suppose I can spare a minute."

A tiny laugh bubbled out of Luska before she bolted downstairs, holding Anya's hand.

"Slow down, you two," the Rebbetzin cried as she tried to keep up.

"Please mind the steps, Madam" urged Anya. "The child's very excited, but you need to take care."

Luska waited by the sitting room doors for the

Rebbetzin to catch up. She flung them open and stood back, studying the woman's face for a hint of what she thought.

The Rebbetzin's eyes widened and her lips parted, but she said nothing.

Luska's excitement wrestled with nervousness. The Rebbetzin's silence was more than she could bear, so after a big gulp of air she asked in a near-whisper, "Do you like what I did, Rebbetzin?"

A look of puzzlement swept over the woman's face as her head darted like a bird, looking from place to place. When she reached the far end of the room, she turned to Luska and Anya standing in the doorway. Anya offered to take the Rebbetzin's arm.

"Madam, I can have everything put back in a flash, if that's what you want."

The Rebbetzin waved her hand. "No, leave it as it is."

"Does that mean you like it, Rebbetzin?"

"I do. I had no idea you were so talented at arranging furniture."

Luska beamed. "Saul helped me."

"Saul?" She looked surprised. "Really? How interesting. Well, I must go now. We shall talk about this later."

Luska felt happier than she had in days. She spent the rest of the afternoon doing her chores on the main floor. The Rebbetzin's comments inspired her to make changes in every room. When the Rebbetzin returned, she walked through the area, with Anya and Luska in tow, to see their progress. She said very little, just a comment here and there, but she sounded very pleased with what had been done. Her inspection ended where it all began, in the sitting room.

"My, how a few simple changes can make such a difference."

"I'm so glad you like it, Rebbetzin. I could do this for you upstairs, too."

"The Rabbi and I will talk about it tonight."

Luska had placed three statuettes on the settee. She picked up her favorite, the girl and dog, and showed it to the Rebbetzin.

"These pieces are too pretty to hide away, but I can't find a place to put them together."

The Rebbetzin examined the figurine. "I do not recall buying this." She turned it upside down and squinted at the mark on the bottom. "It must have been a gift." She handed it back to Luska. "I think you should take all three pieces upstairs to the room where you are staying. See if you can work your magic up there and make it perfect for a little girl."

With Anya's help, Luska pushed the bed away from the wall enough to place the second nightstand in the space. Then they moved the big chair into the corner by the back window, where one could sit and see everything in the room or look out to the garden. Luska saw Anya nod in agreement to their changes before she left, though it puzzled her that Anya didn't seem all that pleased.

More needed to be done. Lala moved the low table with its chair away from the dresser so a grown-up could easily walk around it. Then she placed the lamps on the nightstands and her three figurines on the dresser, which she rearranged a few times until she liked the way they fit together. With her flower vase, centered on the table, the room looked pretty but not finished. After some thought, she knew what was missing—nothing in here truly belonged to her.

Luska hunted through her bundle until she found a square white cloth, which she laid across the tabletop, smoothing out as many wrinkles as she could before replacing the vase.

Exhausted, she sat on the bed, her bundle next to her, and examined her work. It looked just like what the Rebbetzin wanted, a room fit for a little girl like her. She felt pleased. More importantly, she'd proved Saul wrong. She was here to stay, and not downstairs, but in this room,

One more thing needed to be done. She returned to her bundle, sorted her clothing from the rest of the laundry, and folded each garment before carrying the pile to the dresser, where she placed them in the empty top drawer. She rewrapped the remaining items into a ball. It had shrunk enough to fit in the space next to her clothing. Contented, Luska shut the drawer.

The room was finally beginning to feel like hers.

Chapter Twenty-One

After dinner, the Zedeks went upstairs. Luska offered to help Anya clear the table. When Luska tried to carry dishes to the kitchen, Anya blocked her way.

"You are to wait here until I come back for you."

"But why can't I go downstairs?"

Anya set the tray down with enough force to make the dishes rattle. "Because I don't want you sent down there, not until you absolutely must go!"

Luska had never seen the woman angry at all, let alone at her. "I'm sorry," her voice quavered, "I only wanted to help you."

The maid buried her face in her hands. "No, I'm the one who's sorry. You're not responsible for all this, but I'm taking it out on you just the same. Why don't you go to your room and let me finish up here."

"Yes, Miss Anya."

"Before you go," she bent down and took Luska by the shoulders. "You worked hard today and did a fine job."

"Oh, thank you Miss Anya. I very much wanted you to think so."

"I ...I'm proud of you."

Luska reached out for Anya and the two hugged. The woman's arms around her felt so warm and comforting she didn't want the hug to end and it seemed to her that Anya didn't either, for they held onto each other a good long while until Vostok entered the room.

"I've locked up for the night," he said as he started down the stairs. "Good night, Anya. Good night...Lala. Are you coming downstairs?"

"Not yet." Anya straightened her apron. "You've done

enough for one day, Lala. Why don't you go to bed?" She picked up the tray of dishes and carried it to the stairs.

"Before you go, Miss Anya," Luska called out. "May I ask, do you think the Rebbetzin is proud of me, too?"

Anya set the tray on the trolley by the stairs. "I can say she was pleased with your work."

"I'm so happy."

"I'm glad, then." Her smile weakened. "Things will be different for you now."

"Yes, it will be the same as it was with Mama and Papa."

She couldn't tell if Anya was still smiling, for the woman had clamped her hand over her mouth. Her eyes weren't smiling, though.

As Luska walked upstairs, her fingertips trailing across the banister which she had polished to a fine sheen, a sense of peace lifted her with every step. Despite her hard work, she didn't feel at all tired, just excited about her prospects for staying with the Zedeks now. Soon she'd be in her little bedroom at the top of the stairs, now filled with her things – the tulip resting in its vase on the little table, items from her bundle tucked away in the dresser, with the three figurines placed on top of it, like old friends gathered in a garden. What had the Rebbetzin said when she gave the porcelain pieces to her...use them to make the room perfect for a little girl.

It now was.

"Things will be different for you now."

Her heart filled with gratefulness toward the Zedeks. She felt an urge to thank them right now, despite the late hour. The children would be asleep, but the Rabbi and his wife would still be up.

She scampered down the hallway to their bedroom

and paused, ready to knock. The rhythmic squeak of the floorboards leaked through the door and she could picture the Rabbi pacing on the other side.

"...but the girl did a wonderful job today," she heard the Rebbetzin say. "She has proved to be a hard and diligent worker. She is very careful and respectful of our things and she learns quickly. That shows a talent. And she is eager to do even more."

Luska always felt proud to hear Mama and Papa praise her when she did her chores, but hearing the Rebbetzin say it not only filled her heart with pride, but with hope. Hope that she could finally convince the Rabbi to let her stay.

"Where would they get this idea to take her from me?" Luska caught some temper in the Rebbetzin's voice.

"They came to see me today."

"*I talked to the Grossfleischs...I have a meeting scheduled with them....*"

Luska bit her lip.

"So you spoke to them about it, against my wishes?"

"It is our only option, Naomi, and a good one at that, but we must decide soon."

"But why do they want her?"

"They met Lala the other day."

Luska caught her breath. No, this can't be true. The Rebbetzin won't allow it. She can't.

"And now, all of a sudden, they want to take her out of the country? Well, I do not care what they want. I want her to stay with us."

"But why, when—"

"I do not want her to leave." The Rebbetzin's voice grew loud.

She's fighting for me! Luska had to press her hands over her mouth to keep from shouting out in joy. The Rebbetzin won't let those horrible people take me away.

After a period of silence, the Rabbi said, "You do not want her to leave...with them."

"That is true. I do not want them to have her."

"Why not?"

"They do not deserve her."

"Naomi, it has been seven years. Have they not been punished enough?"

"And what difference has it made? They seem to be managing quite well and now have everything they want except for one thing – and I am not going to give it to them."

"Then what about Lala? "

"They do not deserve to be rewarded for what they did. I would rather see her sent to an orphanage. It would be less painful."

"For whom? My dear, if I honor your request, it would also punish her."

"Then let her remain here with us. I need her here. Seeing her gives me hope."

The floorboards began to creak again. A wordless grunt that did not sound happy set Luska's stomach tumbling.

"Hershel, please stop pacing. It makes me queasy."

The squeaking stopped.

"I know you are angry with them for going against your wishes, my dear, but I am asking you to put your personal feelings aside for one moment and consider what would be best for Lala, not only now, but in the future."

Another long pause set Luska's nerves on fire.

"I admit I feel somewhat conflicted about this," The Rebbetzin said.

"Should she not have everything a child needs? They can provide her with so much more than we would be able to, beginning with a fresh start."

Lala fought the urge to cry out, But Rebbetzin, you want me, and that's more important than the Grossfleischs' money, than all the riches in the world.

No response came immediately. Luska shuddered in the silent hallway. Fight for me, Rebbetzin. Who else will?

"I suppose I am being a little selfish. Oh, you have me all confused. I need to think about this more."

Luska could hear him kiss his wife. "That is all I ask. If you do, I promise I will accept whatever you decide."

"I need to think about this more...."

Luska could hardly believe what she'd just heard. She backed away from the door, her hands still pressed against her mouth. There could be no cries of joy, though, only of misery for how her fortunes had changed with a few words.

She ran back to her room and collapsed at the foot of the bed, sobbing. A toss of a coin to decide her future couldn't have been any more unfair, or cruel. Shock turned to despair and her sadness deepened her confusion of the last few days.

The Rebbetzin took his arm. "Hershel, I want to keep her."

Maybe not anymore.

Luska's tears subsided. She cried for so long her head throbbed, but not as much as her heart. She opened the drawer holding her precious possessions and, with trembling hands, rolled each item back into the rest of her laundry. She looked around the room, which hours ago had begun to feel like hers.

"Get out of that bedroom and go back to your village, with your rags and your dirty face and your low class class manners...that bedroom is being saved for someone worthy, and if I do not deserve it, then you certainly do not."

The Rebbetzin thought she was worthy.

"Can we agree to adopt her if nothing else works out," she whispered.

Could the woman who fought so hard to keep her no longer want her?

The Rabbi waved his hand. "Please understand, Lala, I am not convinced this is a good plan. I would still prefer to find a family to adopt you as I promised"

"But in the meantime, you will stay with us." his wife added.

She started panting like a dog in summer. What could have happened between this afternoon, when the Rebbetzin told her to make this room her own, and tonight?

"So you spoke to them about it, against my wishes?"

The Grossfleischs! How could the Rabbi send her away with them? He promised....

"I do not want her to go." The Rebbetzin's voice grew loud.

But what happened to change that?

"I need to think about this more..."

Why would the Rebbetzin agree to let her go to the Grossfleischs? Why, why, why?

"I spent most of the day with them, Mother." Saul piped in.

Saul. This had to have been his idea.

"No one else wanted you."

He'd been right all along. They were going to send her away. She gripped her churning stomach and crumpled onto the chair before she collapsed. A thunderstorm raged in her head. Her thoughts swirled in gusting wind and drowned in pounding rain.

Panting made her dizziness worse. She pressed her forehead against the cool wood of the dresser top and stared into the darkness of the empty drawer below.

"...but Saul, I'm not taking your mother away."

"Yes, you are. She spends more time with you than with me. I have always had to share her, first with David, then Esther, and now you, too...."

Why did Saul have to be so selfish? Why couldn't he share his parents with her, or Esther? Or David...

"But Mother loved him, more than anyone else in the world."

David.

He nodded. "David's finally gone and I have my Mother back, and then you show up, with the same brown hair and dark

144

eyes. And what does Mother do? She puts you in his room, with all of his things, and in his bed."

The Rebbetzin loved that boy. Losing him caused her such pain. Luska understood that all too well.

Yes. It became so clear to her.

That's why she wanted to keep me, why she put me in his room, and in his bed. She wants me to be him, so she can love me like she loved him. Then maybe her pain would go away.

I can make her pain go away.

A flutter ran through her, a sensation as though she were lifted out of her body. She rose up and slid the drawer closed. She watched herself undress and roll each garment back into her bundle, which she placed on the table next to her wilted tulip. Then she went to the dresser and pulled the lower drawer open. The blue velvet suit and stained white shirt came into view.

She took out the jacket first and laid it across the chair. Next she removed the shirt and draped it over the jacket. The pale stains weren't as obvious in the dim light. When she pulled out the pants, something fell to the floor. A small oval disk bordered in silver. A framed picture. She held it up to the light. A boy younger than Saul, dressed in that suit, looked back at her. He resembled the Rebbetzin except he had dark hair, slicked back, and large dark eyes. She laid the picture on the dresser and took the white stockings and black shoes from the drawer.

She dressed slowly, moving as though in a dream. The clothes were a little tight. It took several tugs to button the trousers, but the stockings and shoes fit perfectly.

The photograph reminded her of one more thing that needed to be done to complete the picture. She tore off one of the ribbons from her nightshirt and used it to tie back her hair. Anya was so kind to sew it on for her. She felt badly about ripping it off, but this was for something very important. How else could she persuade the Rebbetzin to let her stay?

Vostok had put out the house lamps, but as Luska approached the couple's bedroom, she saw light glowing along the bottom of the door. She stopped in the toilette to check her appearance, to take one more look at the framed picture before laying it face down on the counter. She kept her head lowered, trembling at the thought of how desperate she felt.

"But Mother loved him, more than anyone else in the world."

What if Saul had lied to her? He would do that. But he didn't lie about this. Luska had learned to tell when people lied. She knew Saul told the truth that night about how his mother felt about her dead son, the boy in the photograph.

Would this work? It had to. It just had to.

She finally lifted her head to face her reflection in the mirror. Her eyes registered surprise. The resemblance was very strong, enough to persuade the Rebbetzin to let her stay. She exhaled and calmed down, for what she saw convinced her that this would work.

Luska had become David.

Chapter Twenty-Two

She stood in front of the bedroom, ready to knock, while a million thoughts raced through her mind; images of happy people welcoming her into the family, of sweet voices, of loving words, of kisses. She touched her cheek. The last person to kiss her there was Papa. Dear Papa. What would he think about all this? She shook the fantasies from her head and with every gram of strength within her rapped on the door.

"Who is it?" The Rebbetzin's voice sounded surprised. Luska said nothing, waited a moment and then knocked once more.

"I am already up, Hershel."

Luska heard footsteps approaching the door.

"What is this...?"

Once the door opened, every breath took an eternity. First the Rebbetzin stared ahead, impatience on her face. She lowered her head until she saw Luska. Her eyes grew wide. Her hands rose to her face. Her mouth gaped open. Luska saw that look once before – at the river bend, on the body of a corpse murdered by Cossacks. A look of total horror.

Then she heard a sound. It began as a rumble from deep inside the woman's belly, growing louder and sharper as it rose to her throat. By the time it left her mouth, it exploded into a bloodcurdling scream that shot through the hallway and filled every corner of the house.

Luska ran from the spot to her room, gasping for air. Distressed cries from every floor echoed in her ears. Not even the servants could help her now. She snatched her bundle and the wilted tulip from its vase and tore down the stairs. She pulled on the front door, but Vostok had locked up for the night. Standing on tiptoes, she stretched her little fingers until they barely reached the door latch. Unable to grab the bar firmly, she kept pushing her fingertips against it, gasping with each attempt to slide it even a little bit, struggling for what seemed like forever to pry it open. As loud voices spilled down from the upper floor, she fought her panic by pushing even harder. The sound of footsteps bounding down the stairs set her heart beating wildly, and with one last push, the lock slid away and clicked open. Her sweaty hands slipped off the handle, but she pulled again with all of her might.

"Lala, stop!"

The Rabbi's voice followed her out the door.

She ran for several blocks before slowing to catch her breath. The dull light of the gas lamps made the city seem a lot more frightening to her. Curtains were drawn and very few lights illuminated the windows in the townhouses. The streets were deserted. A pair of glowing eyes stared at her from a corner of a building. A cat emerged from the shadows and strode past her with its prize, a mouse locked between its jaws, before it streaked away. She continued walking with no sense of where she was or where she was headed, except that it had to be as far away from the Zedek house as possible.

A nearly full moon rose above the rooftops, shining more light on the city, but walking along these unfamiliar streets felt as menacing as wandering through the forest. The night chill finally penetrated her coat of uneasiness. Once again she wrapped herself in Papa's shirt and continued on.

A raspy voice called out, "Hey boy, what are yer doin' out here?"

Fighting her instinct to run, she faced an old man sitting on a stoop, brandishing a walking staff. He bumped a dented metal cup at his side and it jangled. His ragged clothing and unkempt appearance frightened her.

"I'm a stranger, sir," she replied in as deep a voice as she could muster to sound older. "I'm lost. Could you direct me to the town square?"

He leaned forward and squinted at her. "How old are yer, boy?"

Boy? Of course, she still had on David's suit. The man couldn't see very well, so Luska stretched herself upright to appear taller.

"I'm ten," she lied, and bit her lip.

"Why are yer going to the town square at this hour?"

"Um…I…." She struggled to find an answer.

The old man said nothing at first. "Yer runnin away, aren yer? Why else would a fine young man like yerself be out at this ungodly hour?"

She didn't know what to say.

Leaning against his staff, he rose and hobbled a few steps toward her. She backed away.

The man held out his hand. "Yer got any money for a poor beggar like meself?"

"No, sir."

"Not even a kopek?"

She shook her head. "I would give you one if I had it."

"Yer mean to tell me that a fine dressed lad like yerself has no money?"

"I don't, sir, but I have some clothing to trade, if you tell me how to get to the town square." She pulled Papa's trousers from her bundle and held them up.

The old man gave her directions. She tossed the pants over his outstretched arm and ran off.

"It's awful far for a boy like yer to walk, though, more than three kilometers," he hollered after her.

Three kilometers. If he only knew how far I walked last week, she thought.

She hurried on, often glancing back to see if the beggar or anyone else was following her. The echo of a horse-drawn wagon sent her running across the street, and she narrowly missed smashing into a cart parked along the dark road. The

149

sound of splashing water led her to a fountain, and after drinking enough handfuls to revive her, she continued walking until the buildings began to look familiar. She turned the corner and found herself back in the town square.

"You can't be wandering the streets at night, it isn't safe. Why don't you spend the night behind the flower shop and continue your search in the morning."

The building's roof jutted out in back, completely covering a small niche in the stone wall, which provided some protection if it rained or turned windy. Luska got right to work setting up her shelter for the night. A large burlap sack filled with old leaves and stems lay in the space, so she rolled it out a bit to make a fourth wall. Then she made up a bed with items from her ball of laundry. Now all that was left was...she gasped.

"What have I done?"

She crouched against the stone wall and cried so loudly she felt certain someone would come and find her, but no one did.

Time passed. The only sound she heard was her own weeping.

There was nothing to do now but try to sleep. The velvet suit and Papa's shirt should have been enough to keep off the cool night air, but a chill sank into her bones like a winter storm and she couldn't stop shivering. She pulled another cloth from her bundle to wrap around her. As it came out, so did the top half of Mama's dress.

Mama.

She eased the dress out and propped it against the sack, trying to picture Mama in it. Only pieces of memories were clear. Her thick hair, wavy and black. Her dark eyes. The way her growing belly strained against the seams of her old dresses.

Her hand traveled across the worn fabric, past the beet stains she couldn't wash out. She rubbed her fingertip over the

150

bump of thread left behind when Mama's button popped off, sending a rush of fresh tears down her cheeks.

"Mama," she murmured, "oh, Mama."

Pressed against the wall, Luska wrapped the sleeves behind her neck, slipped her arms around the bodice and hugged the empty dress close to her trembling body as she rocked and sobbed, rocked and sobbed.

She sat there until the moon rose high in the night sky. After a while her tears stopped, but the pain and longing remained.

"...each dawn brings a promise new."

The last petal on the tulip dropped off and fell to the street...the tulip given to her by Mr. Prodan.

"Did you think I stole that? The florist is a friend of mine. I will pay him when I return on Monday, so you needn't worry about either of us getting into trouble."

Tomorrow was Monday!

Chapter Twenty-Three

A wagon clattered down the street, waking Luska with a start.

"Where am I," she cried, gawking at the unfamiliar place. Her hand brushed the side of her leg while she struggled to stand. As soon as she felt the damp velvet, she remembered.

Her body ached. Was it from sleeping on the street, or the cold air? It didn't matter. What mattered was that if Mr. Prodan couldn't help her, she might have to sleep here again tonight.

Luska went to the fountain to wash up and then returned to the privacy of her niche to undress. She fought the urge to throw away the suit that led her to her predicament. Instead she wrapped it up with her possessions, but decided to leave on the stockings and shoes. She considered wearing the same gray dress she wore the night Mr. Prodan found her. It would show him nothing had changed since he last saw her...

"The Rebbetzin sighed. "I should find some clothes for Lala before Sabbath."

...and the Rebbetzin made promises she didn't keep.

"Do I look...proper...for dinner?"

"More than proper, you look lovely, Miss."

She put on the dress made by Anya.

Her heart raced as she remembered how Mr. Prodan had come to her rescue. He brought her to the Zedeks believing they would help her. She would tell him what happened, and he'd help her again. Mr. Prodan gave her his word, and he would keep it, too, for Papa's latch saved his life.

Mist cloaked the town in a gloomy haze, but as the

morning clouds lifted, the sky lightened to a pale gray. Gradually, the patter of horse-drawn carriages and rushing people filled the streets. She could hear peddlers' carts parking in the town square, the clanking of metal and the dull thud of shifting crates as they set up for business. The smell of coffee and freshly baked goods drifted over the walls, filling her nose if not her empty stomach. A door swung open several meters from where she stood. The shopkeepers were opening their stores for business, so Luska gathered up her things and headed around the corner.

She recognized the burly shop owner who knew Mr. Prodan. He sat on a crate outside his front window and lit his pipe. She nodded to him as she stood in front of his store. Checking her reflection in the store window, she ran her fingers through her hair and straightened her dress, wanting to look nice for Mr. Prodan. He would tell her how lovely she looked in it....

"Excuse me, child, can I can help you?" the florist puffed on his pipe.

Luska shook her head. "I'm waiting for Mr. Prodan, sir. He's due today."

The florist checked the notebook in his pocket. "You mean his wreath? I was told it had to be ready on Wednesday."

"But he told me Monday."

"They moved Prodan's funeral up to today? What's the hurry? He's only been dead for two days."

Luska felt the blood rush from her body. "Dead...Mr. Prodan is dead?"

The man shook his head.

What a relief, she thought, I knew he was wrong. Mr. Prodan couldn't be dead.

"Terrible shame." He kept shaking his head. "Killed for his cart. Third merchant this month."

"But...but...the latch...he had the latch...."

"That useless thing?" the florist snorted. "Every Cossack is on to that trick now. They even found out where the fellow who made them lived. Went back there and destroyed the town. Killed him and nearly every living thing there, the monsters. A terrible shame, terrible shame...."

The world went gray. Noises from the square rang hollow, like voices under water. Luska managed only a few steps before her feet gave way, and she crumpled to the pavement like a broken doll. A tangle of legs swarmed around her. She didn't know how long she was down, if the sidewalk beneath her was hot or cold, if she was still breathing.

"Lala, are you alright?" A kindly voice broke through.

"What?" Luska gazed up. The man and woman looked familiar.

"Do you remember us? We met you at the Zedeks the other day."

It was the couple who had come to see the Rebbetzin on the Sabbath.

The man extended his hand. "I'm Jakob Hafstein, and this is my wife, Sarah. Let me help you." He got her to her feet. "Did you fall?"

"No, I ...."

"You don't look well." Sarah's palm pressed against her forehead. "Do you feel ill?"

"No, I...I don't feel anything." Her mind spun, jumbling her thoughts.

"What are you doing here? Shouldn't you be home?"

"Home?...home. Yes, that's what I'll do. I'll go home. There's no place for me here."

Sarah linked her arm in Luska's. "We'll take you there. You're in no condition to walk by yourself."

Luska pulled out of her grasp. "Oh no, you can't come with me. It's too far, at least several days walk, but if you could show me where the main road is..." she wobbled toward the alleyway where Mr. Kasyanov had left her.

155

"Jakob, stop her."

"Wait a minute," he caught up to her, "we shall take you to the Zedeks...."

"No, I did something very bad and if I go back, they'll send me away somewhere horrible. I'd rather return to my village and die there, like the rest of them."

Her words upset the man, but she didn't care.

"Don't say that, child," implored Jakob, "I am sure things are not as bad as they seem right now. Let us take you...."

"No, I won't go."

They stood around her, blocking her escape.

"Please, you must come with us." Sarah's voice was firm. "We can't in good conscious let you run off in your condition. Whatever the problem, I'm sure it can be solved."

She didn't want to go, but their faces bore the same expressions as Mama and Papa when they meant business. She realized the Hafsteins would chase her down every street in the city before they'd allow her to flee, and so she relented, at least for now.

The three walked back to the Zedek house. Sandwiched between Jakob and Sarah, Luska refrained from any unnecessary conversation or contact. She refused to let their sense of unease concern her and instead occupied her mind with plans to escape. If the Zedeks wouldn't let them in, she would take the opportunity to run away again, without interference.

Jakob offered his hand. "Would you like me to carry that for you?"

She squeezed her bundle even tighter. "No."

She returned her focus to her escape plan. If the Hafsteins were permitted in, she would escape another way.

"Are you tired, Lala?" Jakob asked. "Would you like to rest awhile?"

"No."

The couple continued to make small talk, which Luska mostly ignored.

Sarah broke the silence. "It must be tough to be orphaned, isn't it, Lala?"

Luska stopped. "How did you know?"

"Dear, you're too angry to be that young and have parents. Why don't you tell us what happened to your family?"

She told them the story of her ordeal in a bland voice, like she was reciting a nursery rhyme. The couple listened and expressed sympathy, but Luska didn't care. She shrugged off the horror on their faces. All the grown-ups who heard her sorry tale looked horrified, but here she was, no better off than the day she fled the burned out ruins that had been her home.

Jakob kept shaking his head. "I am astounded that you survived all that."

"That's what everybody says." She relayed how she learned of Mr. Prodan's death, and the reason behind it.

"You poor thing," Sarah gasped. "First you have no chance to mourn your loss, and then this happens. No wonder you're in such pain."

"No I'm not," she snorted. The idea was ridiculous.

Sarah fished a handkerchief out of Jakob's coat pocket and blotted it against Luska's mouth. "Then why is your lip bleeding?" Dots of red stained the white cloth.

Luska touched her tongue to her lip and felt a warm bead of liquid. She had bitten through the skin without realizing it. She shrugged, "I told you, I don't feel anything."

"Quite understandable for someone in shock." Jakob patted her shoulder. "That often happens when you are faced with something too hard to bear."

"You're wrong. A lot of bad things have happened, but I always felt it before. When I came back to my village and saw what they did to it, I was so scared I could feel my heart go buhbump, buhbump." She thumped her chest to show them what she felt. "When I knew Mama and Papa were gone, my heart felt empty, but it hurt so much I knew it was still there. And when I… I ran away, my heart pounded so loudly it sounded like thunder.

"But when I found out about Mr. Prodan, and why the Cossacks destroyed my home, something else happened to me." She touched her hand to her chest. "Now, I feel nothing." She looked up at them. "My heart must be dead."

That stunned them into silence. Not that it bothered her. Luska needed to finish her escape plans, but a growing curiosity about the Hafsteins distracted her.

Although he towered over his tiny wife, Jakob wasn't very tall, about the same height as the Rebbetzin. He had a smile that made his deep blue eyes twinkle, and when he offered her his hand earlier, she noticed that it was rough, like Papa's. This man worked. Sarah looked like a girl who hadn't finished growing. Her upper body looked squashed down and was mostly bosom. She had a pleasant face with dark eyes, full lips, and hair that reminded Luska of Mama.

"You're staring at me," Sarah admonished. "What do you want to know? Just ask me and I'll tell you if I can."

"You're not like the other people I've met in the city."

"How so?"

"You talk funny. All your words sound different."

"We're from another country. Anything else?"

She still wasn't sure. "And you talked to Mr. Vostok."

"We've known each other a long time. Why are you surprised that I talked to him?"

"Nobody else does, or to Miss Anya. They only tell them what to do. But you talked to him, as if—"

The rattle of coins in a metal cup made her flinch. She fell silent as they passed the ragged man who had bothered her last night. The Hafsteins drew in closer to her, and Sarah placed a protective arm around her shoulder. As soon as they reached the next street, though, Luska shrugged it off. To her surprise, Sarah chuckled at her reaction.

"Lala, you're staring at me again. What is it?"

"Why did you laugh at me?"

"I wasn't laughing at you, I was expressing relief. You showed fear as we passed that beggar. It's the first normal reaction you've had since we found you in the square."

Although she barely knew this woman, Luska suspected Mrs. Hafstein was someone who would always speak her mind, no matter what, but that couldn't explain what compelled Luska to be frank with her.

"I heard Mr. Vostok say your mother died. You looked very sad when he said it and it made me sad, too."

"Of course, losing your mother is very painful, especially for a young girl like you. I understand how you feel, because I lost my mother recently, too. Even though I'm a grown woman with a husband, I still grieve for her and miss her terribly." She took Luska's hand. "Have you been sitting *shiva* for them?"

The ritual of mourning? She shook her head.

"Tch, tch, tch, and him a Rabbi."

Jakob cleared his throat. "Sarah, she's too young. Please let it be."

"Why, do you think we alone have the privilege of their scorn?"

"This is not about us."

As they turned the corner, the Zedek house loomed up against a dull sky. Luska flashed back to the look of horror on the Rebbetzin's face, the wail of anguish that echoed in her ears. Jakob urged her to continue, but she wouldn't budge.

"Please, Lala, come with us and speak to the Zedeks. I assure you whatever happened there last night is not a bad as you think."

"No, you're wrong. If I go back, they'll be very angry, and they'll send me away."

"I do not think so."

159

"Yes they will, just like..." She stared right at him. "...like you. I remember what happened when you came to see the Rebbetzin. She sent you away, too."

"There is no reason to think she will do that to you. Our situation is entirely different."

"She has a point, Jakob. Perhaps you should take Lala there yourself and let me try another path." Sarah winked at him.

"Alright, Sarah two-doors, try it your way."

Jakob cradled Luska's elbow as she walked up the steep steps leading to the door, her bundle wedged at her side. She looked around, but to her dismay Sarah was nowhere to be seen. If the woman could hide so quickly, she must have known Luska wanted to run away. Luckily, Luska thought of another escape plan. Even so, she gnashed her lip as Jakob rang the bell. He waited on the stoop, hands clasped behind his back, like she saw him do last Saturday.

"Mr. Hafstein, why did the Rebbetzin send you away?"

"That is a rather complicated matter." His body slumped as though a great weight dropped on his shoulders. "Truth be told, she was not happy when I married Sarah."

"But why would that matter to the Rebbetzin?"

Jakob sighed deeply. "Because I am her brother."

Chapter Twenty-Four

A rush of panic flooded Luska, and only the fear of Sarah Hafstein hiding somewhere on the street kept her from bolting as the front door to the Zedek home opened. She bit her lip harder, consumed with fear over who would be standing there and what they would do when they saw her.

Vostok nodded to Mr. Hafstein. He looked tired and drawn, but when he saw Luska, his face lit up and his stiff formality melted away.

"Oh thank heavens, you found her! I'm so grateful to you for bringing her back, we were terribly worried. Please come in."

"Perhaps you should check with the Rebbetzin first?" Jakob looked uncomfortable.

"She's not home, sir. Neither is the Rabbi; however I expect them back very soon. Do come in." He escorted them to the sitting room, as he did that first night with Mr. Prodan. Poor Mr. Prodan.

Luska couldn't help staring, as much in surprise as disappointment. The house no longer seemed beautiful to her, despite all the pretty things that filled every room.

She stopped in front of the painting of the Rebbetzin. The woman on the canvas, with the kind face, the confident pose, the understanding glow, was not the same woman Luska faced last night. Mr. Hafstein slipped his arm around her shoulder to urge her on.

Vostok opened the sitting room doors and invited them in with a sweep of his hand. Luska gasped when she entered. Everything had been put back the way it was before, the chairs, the pretty chest with the patchwork lid, even the three pieces the Rebbetzin had given her were once again scattered among the tables. Her hard work, her very presence in the house had been wiped clean.

Jakob picked up the figurine of the young girl holding the dog and chuckled. "My sister once had a dog very much like this one."

Luska ran her finger across the top of the patchwork chest. "This is too nice to be hidden in the corner."

Jakob tipped his head. "Thank you."

"For what?"

"Turn the latch on the front piece and see what happens." He had that twinkle in his eyes again.

She looked to Vostok, who nodded with a slight smile. She twisted the metal key and the piece flipped open, forming a flat surface extending from the body of the chest.

"How did you know it would do that?"

Jakob grinned. "Because I built it."

"You did? Why, it's the most beautiful thing in the whole room!"

"Thank you again."

She wanted to ask him so many questions, but that would further delay her mission. She needed an excuse to slip away, one that wouldn't cause suspicion.

"Would you like some coffee or tea while you wait, sir? And perhaps some milk for the child?" Vostok asked.

"Nothing for me, thanks, but Lala might like something."

This was her chance. "I'm hungry."

"Oh my, have you had your breakfast yet? I will fetch something—"

She held her bundle against her with crossed arms. "No, I should go down to the kitchen and get myself something to eat." Vostok started to protest but she reminded him, "I'm not a guest in this house anymore."

His face fell when she said that. It launched a pang of

guilt, but what choice did she have? Dashing from the room, she flew down the stairs, intent on leaving through the servant's entrance and running off before anyone realized she was gone.

A creaking sound came from the storeroom. She paused by the kitchen door to listen closer, but the sight of food beckoned her to the shelves. She wondered if that noise might have come from her empty belly. The temptation to take some bread and fruit nearly overpowered her. The shelves were beyond her reach, though, and nothing had been left on the plankwood table. It reminded her of the table at home, where she and her parents ate their meals. She would miss fresh bread at breakfast and meat for supper every night, but not much else.

Another creak from the storeroom snapped her back. Luska peered into the room. Most of the crates and bags had been moved alongside the right wall to make space for a small cot and chest of drawers set against the left side. Gray light filtered through the window in the back door just a couple of meters across the floor. With one arm cradled around her bundle, she headed for her escape route and her freedom.

"And just where do you think you're going?"

Luska whipped around. There, on a stool in the back corner of the room, sat Anya. She stared at Luska with silent concern, her lips pressed together, for she hadn't barked out that question. Luska heard the rhythmic patter of a shoe against the wood floor, but it wasn't the Rabbi pacing.

She squeezed her bundle against her body as her teeth clamped down on her lip. Standing next to Anya, with arms crossed and foot tapping the floorboards, reeking of impatience, was her inquisitor – Sarah Hafstein.

Chapter Twenty-Five

"You haven't answered my question." Sarah's tapping boomed in the quiet storeroom like a ticking clock, counting out the seconds as she waited for an answer.

All of Luska's cleverness deserted her. She wouldn't admit she was going to run away, but for some reason she could not bring herself to lie to this tiny woman. Instead, she chose to remain silent.

"Anya told me what happened last night," Sarah continued. "I understand what led you to run away, but she assured me the Zedeks are not angry with you."

She thought of the Rebbetzin's face; of how she screamed, and found it hard to believe the family would ever forgive her for her foolish act.

"Did you know Rabbi Zedek and Vostok were out half the night looking for you?" Sarah circled behind her, blocking the back door.

"No."

"They were worried sick when they couldn't find you."

Luska bit her lip. I have to get away, but how?

Sarah locked the servant's door and asked, "Will you talk to the Zedeks now?"

Luska shook her head. "Nothing has changed, or else you would have told me they weren't going to send me away with the Grossfleischs."

"I see." Sarah's eyes roamed to the cot, then back to Luska. "What if I told you they weren't planning to send you away with them?"

Luska crossed her arms. "I don't know if I could believe that."

Anya forced a smile. "I can truthfully say neither the Rabbi nor Madam ever mentioned the Grossfleischs in their plans."

"But I heard the Rabbi tell her to send me far away. She didn't want to, but then she said she would think about it. It doesn't matter, because she won't want to keep me anymore, not after what I did." Luska thought about the beggar and wondered which fate would be worse.

"It's not my business, or Anya's, to tell you of their plans." The stern tone left Sarah's voice. "You need to discuss this with the Rabbi and his wife. Tell them how you feel. If you want, my husband and I would be happy to stay and help you in any way we can."

"How can you help me when they won't even let you into the house? You had to sneak in downstairs."

Sarah tapped her foot harder, which emboldened Luska. "Mr. Hafstein told me he was the Rebbetzin's brother. Maybe the only reason Mr. Vostok let him in was because no one was home to send him away."

Sarah's face reddened, but at least her tapping ceased.

Anya leaned into the hallway. "I hear footsteps outside. Madam must be back." She wiped her hands on her apron. "I have to go. You know the way out." She hurried upstairs, leaving Luska to stare into the sullen face of Sarah.

"You still intend to run away." Sarah lifted herself onto the stool Anya had just vacated. "Tell me, where will you go, with no money, no food and no way to travel?"

"Far away from here." That was all Luska was willing to admit.

"You mean, back to your village, don't you? 'I'll go home, there's no place for me here,' that's what you told us. Isn't that so?"

What a strange effect this woman had on her. Sarah's insistent gaze and honesty compelled Luska to be truthful. She nodded.

"I wouldn't have believed it, but after all their horrible crimes, you want to help the Cossacks."

What? How could she say that?

"No I don't." She pretended to be indifferent to the woman's remarks, but she could feel steam rising within her.

"But you must, for you're acting like you do."

"I'm not," Luska declared in a much firmer tone.

Sarah mocked, "I don't know if I can believe that."

Luska scowled at the woman, her temper sparked by Sarah's taunting.

Now Sarah crossed her arms. "Do you know what I think? I think you really want to help the Cossacks win their battle."

"No, it's not true!" Luska exploded. "How could you say that, after what they did? They killed Mama and Papa, everyone in my shtetl, and then they killed Mr. Prodan, too. I would never help them, never, never, never. I hate them!" She shook with a fiery rage. "I hate them, I hate them," she said over and over until her shouting faded to a faint mewl.

Sarah slid off the stool and rested a hand on her shoulder. "Feel better now?"

Strangely enough, Luska did feel better. She drew in a deep breath to calm herself before she spat out, "I don't want the Cossacks to win."

"But don't you see that's exactly what will happen if you return to your village?"

"Why do you say that?"

"Because if you go back there you won't survive, which was their intention when they attacked your village." Sarah wagged her finger. "Remember what the florist told you – they wanted to kill everyone to punish your Papa for inventing his latch. That's what they tried to do, but they didn't succeed."

"They didn't?"

"No, my dear, they haven't. At least not yet, because

you're still alive." She cupped Luska's chin. "If you go back, you'll surely die, and they will win. But if you live, then they'll fail, and if you live a long and happy life, despite everything, then they will fail miserably."

The woman's words finally broke through to Luska. How could she go back now? All of her plans drained away like water down a hole.

"I don't know what to do," she moaned.

"Talk to the Zedeks again. Find out what plans they have for you. Mr. Hafstein and I will be there to help you."

"You would do that for me?"

Sarah smiled, and her face lit up like the sun.

"Yes, Lala, we both would."

"I believe you."

"Good. But remember, it's your life, your future. Only you can make the decision."

"I don't want to be sent away with anyone. I want to stay here."

Luska thought she saw a troubled look cross Mrs. Hafstein's face, but it vanished quickly.

"Talk to them before you make up your mind."

She knew Mrs. Hafstein was right, but she wasn't sure she could face the Zedeks after last night. Was it possible she would be forgiven, that the family would welcome her back? She was ready to do more chores, whatever was necessary. Chores. All the work she did in the sitting room – what would it take?

She turned to Sarah. "If I did go upstairs, would you be allowed in, too?"

"That's a good question." Sarah raised an eyebrow. "Did Mr. Hafstein tell you why we're not welcome in this house?"

"He said the Rebbetzin wasn't happy when he married you. Is it because you have this way of making people always tell the truth or that you're very bold for a woman?"

168

She laughed. "Bold you say? Well, I guess I am bold, but you don't know the half of it." A sigh dismissed her humor.

Luska took Sarah's hand. "I'll go upstairs and talk to the Rebbetzin, but only if you come with me."

"Of course I will, but let's get you something to eat first. You must be starving."

Sarah took her to the kitchen where Luska quickly devoured two rolls with butter and jam. Sarah straightened up the kitchen afterward and went to the stairs, but Luska tugged her toward the hall.

"No, this way. We're going outside and up the front steps," she insisted. "If they won't let you in, I'm not going in, either."

Sarah beamed. "Look who's bold now. Very well, we'll try it your way."

Hand in hand, they left through the servant's door and walked to the front entrance.

"Mrs. Hafstein, how did you know I would try to run away?"

"I didn't until I heard you running down the stairs."

Luska let go of Sarah's hand. "But you were downstairs with Miss Anya. If you weren't waiting to catch me, why did you come in through the servant's entrance?"

"Why do you think Mr. Hafstein calls me 'Sarah two-doors.'"

They climbed the stairs and Sarah rang the front doorbell. As they waited, she asked, "Still feeling bold?"

Luska pressed her hand against her chest. "My heart is pounding."

Sarah laughed. "Is this the same heart you thought was dead? Well, well, well. Looks like you and I have brought it back to life. Not bad for a couple of bold girls."

Chapter Twenty-Six

Vostok escorted Luska and Sarah to the sitting room and opened the doors. The Rebbetzin lounged on the settee as she chatted with her brother. She looked happy and relaxed; her eyes were bright and her skin glowed, both flattered by the lavender dress she wore.

"More tea, Jakob," she asked. "Or perhaps you would like a glass of brandy to celebrate your good news." Her cheery smile heartened Luska. Maybe Mrs. Hafstein was right.

Jakob extended his cup. "Tea is fine."

At the flick of the Rebbetzin's hand, Vostok took the tea pot from its serving tray on the sideboard and refilled Jakob's cup before leaving the room with a nod to Luska and Sarah.

Jakob then noticed the two standing in the open doorway. "Ah, there you are."

The Rebbetzin cast a cool glance at Sarah and Luska and turned away.

Jakob dropped a lump of sugar into his cup. "Naomi, you remember my wife, Sarah."

"Of course. Please, come in and join us." She put on a polite face. Sarah gave a gracious nod and took the chair next to her husband. Luska's confidence faded and she remained back until the Rebbetzin silently motioned her in with the same flick of the hand she'd just given Vostok. Luska would have preferred sitting away from the Rebbetzin's glare, but all the chairs faced the settee. She took the seat next to Sarah, who reassured her with a quick pat on the hand. The Rebbetzin sat up even straighter than usual and directed her gaze away from them. Luska squirmed in her seat, thinking nothing could be worse than this.

She cleared her throat. "Rebbetzin, I...."

Her words disappeared with her breath as the woman turned to face her. Hope for forgiveness was ended by Rebbetzin's expression, as dark and icy as any Luska had seen on Saul's face. She shriveled back into her seat with the knowledge that this was much worse than being ignored. She turned to Sarah, desperate for a clue. Sarah's glare, directed at the far wall, could have sliced the room in two, but the bold woman held her tongue.

"What were you saying, Lala?" Jakob's gentle voice relaxed her.

"I wanted to say I'm sorry to the Rebbetzin for what I did last night. I truly didn't mean to scare her."

"I realize that now." She spoke directly to Jakob. "I cannot imagine why she would do something like that."

Steam rose from Jakob's cup as he swirled a spoon through the amber liquid. "Oh? Then perhaps Lala should explain her reason."

"Because when I went to your room to thank you last night...I didn't mean to listen, but when I heard you talking about me, I did." She added in a near-whisper, "The Rabbi said he wanted to send me away. You didn't want him to, but when you said you'd think about it—"

"You decided to dress up as my dead son?" The Rebbetzin's voice cracked.

"Naomi, this was all an innocent mistake," Jakob chided. "She overheard part of your conversation and took it out of context. All she wanted—"

"I know what she wanted." Naomi's face twisted up into a knot and she began to tremble. "But some things cannot be had, no matter how badly you want them, or how hard you fight, or how much you pray!" She exploded into tears and wailed so hard her body shook.

Jakob hurried to his sister's side. He took her hand and stroked her back. "She did not have it in mind to upset you."

He repeated it several times, but the Rebbetzin still wailed.

Sarah rushed to her, too. "Let me get you a glass of water, or would you prefer something stronger?"

The Rebbetzin waved her hand weakly. "Water, please."

"I'll ring for Vostok." Sarah patted her hand.

As the Hafsteins fussed over Naomi, Luska stood back, helpless, her heart in knots as she thought about how much pain she had caused. The Rebbetzin's tears were for David, but her words also spoke of how Luska felt about losing Mama and Papa.

Vostok handed the Rebbetzin a glass.

"Drink it slowly," Sarah advised.

The Rebbetzin's head was down, but her eyes darted between the Hafsteins as she sipped water. They took turns stroking her back, patting her hand, and offering words of comfort.

"Take deep breaths."

"Drink a little more, dear."

"There, there."

Luska noticed Vostok waiting at the doorway, unaffected by the Rebbetzin's hysterics. She'd seen that face before. Not on him though, but on the villagers in her shtetl as they listened to Mr. Chelmsky repeat a story heard many times before.

The Rebbetzin handed her empty glass to Sarah. She took it to Vostok, who whisked it away. His expression must have registered with Sarah as well, for when she sat down again, her look of concern had changed to a dark glare.

Naomi sniffled back her last tears. "I have been very emotional lately. Hershel explained that dressing in David's clothes was a misguided attempt to endear herself to us." "Endear" came out sharper than the other words.

Jakob offered his handkerchief to his sister. "My apologies. It was not my intention to upset you; I was trying to help Lala. I did not consider how her actions might have dredged up painful memories."

Naomi dabbed her eyes. "No, how could you? After all, you have never had a child."

Sarah looked about to say something, but she held her tongue.

Jakob returned to his seat. "And you do, so you know how children can do foolish things sometimes. Do you think you could forgive Lala her 'misguided attempt?'"

Naomi's radiant smile spoke before she did. "Of course I can. What kind of mother would I be otherwise? In fact, I have made my decision about that matter we were discussing, and I have decided the girl will stay here, with us."

Luska leapt from her chair, as much from surprise as delight.

"Oh, I'm so happy. Thank you, Rebbetzin…I knew you wouldn't send me away!"

"Lala is pleased with your decision." Jakob caught Luska's hand and drew her over. "Do you want to stay here with the Zedeks?"

"Oh yes, Mr. Hafstein, more than anything."

Sarah lowered her head and her polite smile vanished.

"Very well, I am glad that the matter is settled." Jakob didn't look glad, though. He stood and offered his arm to his wife, but she remained in her seat.

"We should go, Sarah, we still have to take care of that matter in town."

She didn't get up or answer him. Instead she faced the Rebbetzin. "I'm curious. You say you want the girl to stay with you, but in what capacity?"

The question took Luska aback. Even Mr. Hafstein looked bewildered. Why would his wife make trouble now that everything had ended so happily?

"She wants me to stay here, Mrs. Hafstein. She wants me to be hers. That's why she put me in the front bedroom, and let me do chores, so I could be a part of the family." Luska didn't say "like David," for mentioning his name might upset the Rebbetzin. "That's what I want, too."

She turned to the Rebbetzin. "I should have known you wouldn't let the Rabbi send me away. You wanted me all along. I heard you tell him you wanted to keep me the night I first came here."

Sarah's glare never left Naomi. "If that's so, then why, the very next day, did you ask the Sisterhood to help you find her another home?"

"Hershel didn't think it would be a good idea for her to stay, but as the girl can tell you, I promised him I'd make inquiries with the women if he would wait until after the Sabbath to make a decision."

"It's true, I heard them say that," Luska informed Mrs. Hafstein.

Sarah nodded, but her eyes narrowed. "I suppose that's why you persuaded your husband to keep her from attending services at the synagogue...if the congregation actually met this darling girl, they might want to take her in."

Naomi looked pleased, as if she answered a question right.

"And instead of buying the child some decent clothes, you agreed when they suggested giving her donations from the poor box. Is that how you treat one of your own?"

"Sarah, please," Jakob implored. "I know you are disappointed—"

"I'm only thinking of Lala's welfare, Jakob."

The Rebbetzin bristled. "I never took a thing from the poor box for her."

"That's true," Lala exclaimed. "It was Saul who did it."

"Wherever you heard such ridiculous tales, Sarah, you give it more credit than it is due," Rebbetzin said.

"Dear, when I want to find out information, I don't ask the gentry, I talk to their servants."

The Rebbetzin's tightened face looked as sour as Saul's. "I would never lower myself to listen to idle gossip from anyone, let alone such...such unreliable and untrustworthy sources."

"You'd be surprised. They're the ones who know what's really going on, like who's carousing, who's in debt...who's expecting."

The Rebbetzin lost her composure for a moment before snarling, "I will tell you once again, my intention was to keep her."

"You've said that over and over, but you haven't answered my question—keep her as your daughter, or something else?"

"As a member of, of this family."

A cold chuckle escaped from Sarah. "Then why was she doing your housework?"

Jakob put his cup down with such force a wave of tea sloshed into the saucer. "Is this true, Naomi? Were you training her for household service?"

The Rebbetzin's smile had disappeared with Sarah's question, but Jakob's response jolted her. She fussed with her kerchief, tucking stray hairs under the knot, and avoided his stony gaze.

"I began her training with Anya only after I explained everything to her, and she agreed. In fact, she told me she wanted to do it," she finally sputtered.

"She is a child. How could you condemn her to a life in service, doing housework, especially when you knew there is a family interested in adopting her?" Jakob pressed.

Luska's stomach twisted at the thought of being taken in by the Grossfleischs. "The Rebbetzin wanted me to do chores, not housework, Mr. Hafstein. Miss Anya and Mr. Vostok do the housework."

"And what is the difference between chores and housework, Lala?" Sarah asked.

Luska's stomach tumbled more. She wondered about that, too. But it didn't matter as long as the Rebbetzin wanted her back. Everything would be fine if the Hafsteins would stop interfering. The Rebbetzin had fought hard for her and won. Now Luska had to fight for the Rebbetzin. Luska jumped up and stood beside her.

"Why are you doing this?" Luska demanded of Sarah. "You told me this was my decision and I have decided I want to stay here. If you don't stop quarreling she might change her mind again and send me away."

"Lala, do you understand why the Rebbetzin wants you to stay?" asked Sarah.

She looked up at the Rebbetzin "Yes, it's because you want me. You wanted to keep me ever since that first night...even when the Rabbi said I'd be disrup...disrupt...?"

"Disruptive?" Jakob picked up the figurine of the girl with the dog and chuckled softly. "I noticed this before. It reminded me of the little white dog you wanted so dearly when we were children. Remember?" He handed it to his sister. "Father said the same thing, little dogs yip and snap and chew on everything, but you begged and pleaded until he gave in. What was that dog's name?"

She barely glanced at the figurine. "I do not remember."

"Neither can I, but I do recall you eventually decided Father was right, and got rid of him after he destroyed one of your favorite shoes."

The Rebbetzin roughly deposited the figurine on the nearest table. Luska scooped it up, fearing it might fall and break. She used the skirt of her fine dress to rub the porcelain piece clean, as she'd been taught, and then placed it on a table next to one of the other figurines.

Sarah clutched her chest and groaned.

Luska picked up the third piece and added it to the arrangement. "They should be together," she explained as she shifted them around. When they looked agreeable she returned to the settee. "Rebbetzin, you said the other day I could keep those pieces upstairs in my room. Now that I'm staying may I put them back?"

"Wait until after the Hafsteins leave," she told her.

"Because you wouldn't want Lala to find out about the new quarters you've arranged for her until it was too late, would you," Sarah insisted.

"…make your room perfect for a little girl…."

Luska flashed to the little cot and dresser in the storeroom, but that couldn't be for her.

The Rebbetzin didn't answer. No one spoke. At last, Mr. Hafstein broke the silence.

"Lala, what exactly did you hear the Zedeks discuss yesterday that made you decide to put on David's clothes?"

"I heard the Rabbi say he wanted to send me far away, to another country…with the Grossfleischs." She wriggled her face in disgust.

"Hershel never said that," insisted Naomi. "His meeting with them had nothing to do with her."

"But Rebbetzin, he said he met with some people, and that's when he decided to send me away. You kept saying no, but then you said you'd think about it." Luska's stomach wrenched as she remembered. "I was so afraid you'd say yes. Then you told him, 'I suppose I am being a little selfish.' I don't understand. Why would it be selfish to keep me?"

Jakob and Sarah had a wordless talk with their eyes. Then he turned to face his sister, looking as stern as his wife.

"Are you going to tell her, or do we?"

The Rebbetzin crossed her arms and exhaled. "The Rabbi spoke with my brother and his wife about adopting you." She spoke over Luska's head. "They expressed some interest, but they live in another country, so a decision must be made quickly."

Luska stared at the Hafsteins. "You? You're the family

that wants to adopt me?"

Jakob smiled. "We are."

"Mr. Hafstein and I always wanted a family. And then a childless couple hoping for a child meets an orphan who needs parents. What could be better?"

"All you have to do is say yes. Please say yes, Lala."

"But why would you want to do that, Mr. Hafstein? You hardly know me."

Sarah smiled. "We adore you…"

"We felt that way from the moment we met you last Sabbath," added Jakob.

"…and with time I know we will grow to love you."

Luska's experience with the Zedeks left her doubtful. "How can you be so sure?"

Sarah cupped Luska's chin. "Because you're easy to love."

"…I know we will grow to love you…."

Could they? Luska once hoped it would happen, but everything she'd been through taught her to be cautious. Sarah's earnestness made it hard to doubt her, but still….

"Won't I disrupt your family? That's what the Rabbi said would happen."

"Lala, you wouldn't disrupt our family, you'd create it. Without you, we're just a husband and wife, but with you, we are a family."

A family, like with Mama and Papa. She turned to the Rebbetzin. "And you don't want me to go with them. You want me to stay with you." Luska reached out for a hug, but the woman folded her arms. Was she still angry about last night? There was no anger in her eyes. They looked through Luska as though she wasn't there, like she was a window, or worse, a smudge that needed to be wiped clean. Luska had seen her look at Saul that way; Esther, too. Without love, or kindness…or pain.

Her eyes were open but her heart was shut.

The Rebbetzin shrugged. "I would prefer that you to stay here, with us...and train for service."

"So I could stay here?"

"As a servant," added Jakob.

"There is nothing wrong with being in service." Naomi cast a defiant glare at Sarah. "Just ask your wife."

Sarah returned her gaze with equal vigor. "It's preferable to starving or begging, and more honorable than other pursuits, but I can assure you, no one ever chooses to enter into service unless there is no other choice." She beckoned Luska over. "Now that you know the truth, what do you want to do? Stay here and become a servant, or come live with us, as our daughter?"

A daughter. This is what she wanted, what she had with Mama and Papa, but lost.

"Hershel, I want to keep her."

"I want that, too, Rebbetzin." She murmured to herself.

What she thought she could have with the Rabbi and his family, which she also lost.

"I would prefer that you to stay here, with us...and train for service."

What would she do if it happened again with the Hafsteins, if they changed their mind?

"...a childless couple hoping for a child meets an orphan who needs parents...."

But she wasn't a child. What if she stayed with the Zedeks instead? She'd have no real home...no family...no one to love... and no one to lose.

Luska smiled. "I've decided."

Jakob nodded. "Wonderful. We should..."

"I want to stay here with the Rebbetzin."

The Hafsteins were taken aback. Even Naomi looked surprised by her decision.

Sarah shook her head. "Don't you want a home and a family, parents to love you?"

180

"I'd rather stay with the Rebbetzin. I'm very sure."

"But Lala, you must understand that if you stay here, it won't be as a daughter, but as a servant, like Miss Anya, working morning to night. You will never have an opportunity to go to school, learn to read and write, or grow up to be anything other than a housemaid in service. After everything you've been through, why would you want to give up your chance for a real future, with us?"

Luska shrugged. "I don't mind doing chores." She sat next to the Rebbetzin to show her appreciation. "Everyone treats me like a child, except you. Remember what you told me in your bedroom last Sabbath, that I'm not a little girl anymore?"

"I did say that to you. That was when I first thought about letting you train for service." She stood and began pacing the room, like the Rabbi always did. Her eyes watered. She stopped at the chest with the figurine of the girl and the dog. "Well, now that everything has been settled, we should let her get back to her training."

Jakob looked very sad. "We ought to go, Sarah." He offered her his arm.

The brightness in Sarah's expression had gone out. "You're right, dear. We've much to do."

Naomi held the sitting room doors open for them. "Thank you for returning her."

Luska ran to the doors. "And thank you for everything you did for me. Will you come back and visit?"

"Probably not, Lala. I am sorry." Jakob stroked her cheek.

Luska was sorry too. They were very nice, even if they couldn't understand her decision. She'd miss them. But she had learned over the past week that too often the things that you want the most, that are dearest to you, are the ones you can't have.

Chapter Twenty-Seven

The Rebbetzin and Luska escorted the Hafsteins to the front door.

Jakob snapped his fingers. "Raja." He smiled at his sister.

"What?"

"Raja. That was the name of your little dog."

"No, it was something else, something similar. I cannot remember."

"It was a long time ago." He adjusted the brim of his hat. "I always thought the only reason you wanted that dog was because Father said you could not have it."

"I wanted it even before I asked him to buy it for me...one of the other girls in my class wanted it, too...." Her brow furrowed. "Why is it that I cannot remember its name?"

"We tend to forget what is not important to us."

"Mother would have remembered." A pained smile passed her lips. "Sometimes I thought she loved that dog more than me. Do you remember how livid she was when I gave it away?"

They stopped near the front door. Sarah gestured to a family portrait hanging on the wall over a side table.

"What a lovely picture. You have a beautiful family, Naomi."

"Thank you."

Sarah picked up a silver framed photograph from the table. "Is this David?"

"Yes." The Rebbetzin's voice was soft.

"Such a fine looking boy."

The Rebbetzin took the picture from Sarah and held it in both hands. "David was remarkable. Sometimes you sense these things as a child develops, but with my son, I knew it from the moment he was born...handsome, personable. bright...someone who would grow up to be a remarkable man."

Her hands trembled slightly as she seemed to study every line and shadow of the photograph. "Everything about him was unique, even the disease that took him from us. Did you know it only affects Jewish children? They usually develop the symptoms in infancy, but David showed no signs until after his second birthday, which is very rare."

Her fingertips stroked along the frame's edge. "He lived another three years. The last was almost unbearable. I actually thought I would be relieved when it was finally over, but I was wrong. When I lost him, I lost a part of my heart that has never healed. It never will."

Luska looked at the photograph. "Saul told me you loved David more than anything."

Her focus stayed on the picture. "He is right."

Jakob patted his sister's shoulder. "And that is why the child dressed in his clothes, Naomi. Not to hurt you, but to remind you of how she has suffered as well, which only you can end. It is not too late to save her."

The Rebbetzin kept staring at the picture.

Luska never saw the woman as sorrowful as she did now.

"...how she has suffered as well...."

Mr. Hafstein was right. She, too, lost a part of her heart which would never heal. It filled her with a great longing, and she could not speak for fear that she'd start crying and never stop. The more she tried not to feel, the more she felt.

The Rebbetzin put the picture back on the table and went to the front door.

Luska burst out, "I didn't put on David's clothes just to stay, Rebbetzin. I did it because I wanted you to love me as much as you loved him."

184

"I could never love another child as much as I loved David!"

A whimper came from the breakfast room. Standing in the doorway, Saul began to cry. He covered his ears and ran to his room.

The Rebbetzin exhaled, but didn't follow the boy upstairs. She looked more embarrassed than sorry. "I know what you must be thinking," she told her brother, "but Hershel is far better at handling these situations, much like Father was in that way."

Jakob said nothing.

Her eyes flared. "Rags. The dog's name was Rags."

"You remembered."

"Raja was the doll Mother took away from me as punishment for getting rid of him. She did not speak to me for a week after that. She would not even look at me." Tears rolled down her cheeks as she glanced back at the empty stairway. "What kind of mother has to struggle to love her children?"

Luska patted her arm. "Please don't cry, Rebbetzin. You were right. I thought if you had David back, you wouldn't hurt so much. And if you could love me like you loved him, then maybe I could love you as much as I loved Mama. But I understand now. You showed me it's better to close your heart than to have it hurt all the time."

The Rebbetzin must have understood, too, for their eyes locked. It upset Luska to see all that pain raining down on her. The woman covered her face with her hands and groaned. When her hands dropped, the pain had been replaced with stone determination.

"Hershel was right—I am being selfish." She picked up Luska and put her in Jakob's arms. "Take her."

"Are you sure?"

"Absolutely. Go. Go now, quickly!"

Luska tried to twist around. "Rebbetzin, what are you saying?"

185

"You are going to live with my brother and his wife. They will become your parents."

"But Rebbetzin, I want to stay with you! Please! Why are you sending me away?"

"Because, Lala, you deserve better." She hurried away upstairs.

Sarah pulled front door open wide.

"Nooooooo!" screamed Luska as Jakob carried her out of the house.

Chapter Twenty-Eight

"Let me go, let me go!" Luska kicked and struggled until Mr. Hafstein set her down, but he held onto her. His face turned bright red.

"Promise me...you will not...run away." He puffed between gasps of breath.

She threw him a defiant look, but said nothing.

Vostok hurried down the front steps. "Mr. Hafstein? You wouldn't want to leave without this."

In the confusion, they'd forgotten her bundle. Cradling it in her arms, Luska hugged it to her chest.

"Thank you!" She tucked it under her arm and took Vostok's hand, silently pleading for him to take her back into the house. He patted her hand before releasing it.

"Goodbye, Miss. I wish you every happiness."

He glanced at the front steps and then walked to the side of the house.

Luska watched him go away with sadness in her heart as each step took him further from her as well as from what she most wanted – to return to the safety of the Zedek house.

When he disappeared down the path to the servant's entrance, she sat on the bottom step. "Will Mr. Vostok get in trouble for using the front entrance?"

"I don't think so," Sarah assured her.

"Can't I please go back with him?"

Sarah threw up her hands. "What is it about that house that would make you choose to stay there? It doesn't make sense."

"It does to her, Sarah." Jakob's face still looked very red. "Lala, I can appreciate the feelings you have for the

Rebbetzin, but she has told you plainly she will not love you in the way you want her to, and you cannot change that."

"I know, that's the reason why I want to stay," insisted Luska.

Jakob squatted down to face her eye to eye.

"Do you love her that much?"

She shook her head.

"Then what is it?"

"I feel safe there."

"Safe from what? Cossacks? Poverty? Is it their fine home you do not want to leave?"

"No, Mr. Hafstein."

"Then what are you afraid of?"

"I'm not afraid! I just want the hurting to stop."

Luska saw they did not understand. "When I came back from the river and saw what happened to my shtetl, my home...Mama and Papa...I, I hurt so much I didn't think I could hurt any more. Then I was brought here and the Rebbetzin...she wanted to keep me...she said so. It made me happy that she wanted me, even if no one else did, and I didn't hurt so much. But then she didn't want me to be her little girl anymore."

Mrs. Hafstein clutched her chest again. "That must have been very painful for you."

She nodded. "Then I found out about Mr. Prodan and why my village was attacked...so now I think it's better not to care about anyone." She watched the color drain from Jakob's face.

"And you think a life in service will protect you from your sorrow?" he asked.

She shrugged. "If I work hard and do my chores, I'll have a roof over my head and food on the table. What more do I need? And if I have to do chores, I can do them here with Miss Anya and Mr. Vostok. I have to do something, because if I don't work, I'll be poor and have to take charity. I can't do that, it's not our way."

"Who told you that?" The fire had returned to Sarah.

"It's what the people in my shtetl always said — 'If you have nothing to do, it means you have nothing.'"

"I know that saying, but that's not what it means." Sarah clucked her tongue. "It has nothing to do with being rich or poor. It means that you must have a purpose in life, a reason for living."

Luska didn't believe it, didn't want to believe she'd been wrong, but when she looked at Sarah's face, she could tell the woman was speaking the truth.

"Do you really think that after all you've been through, your purpose is to clean houses for the gentry?" Sarah continued. "I don't think God spared you so you could scrub floors. He must have bigger plans for you, something wonderful. Doesn't that make sense?"

It did, which astounded Luska. Everything she did, everything she tried to do, was because of what she believed to be true, and no one up until now had told her any differently.

Or had they?

"Did you let her go?" Papa asked.

Mama nodded.

"I wish she didn't have to." He gulped down his tea.

Mama took the glass and handed him his bread. "I wish she didn't want to."

"My Mama and Papa tried to tell me, but I didn't understand."

"From what you've told us, they must have needed you to help with the chores even if they weren't happy about it."

"Is that why they argued all the time? Because of me?"

"No, dear, it wasn't you they argued about, only that they had to rely on you so much. Your parents would have preferred to take care of you rather than have you work so hard. Any parent would want that for their child. But now you have the opportunity to live the life your parents wanted for you."

She thought about Mama and Papa.

She piped up, "Let me do the laundry, Papa."

"No, Luska, I've already told you this is not a chore for a child."

"But I'm not a little girl anymore," she insisted. "I want to help, I can do more things for you and Mama, if you'll let me."

"I know, and I appreciate all you've done, but don't be in such a hurry to grow up."

"Don't you think that would make them happy?" Sarah tugged at Luska's hand, but she remained seated.

"Maybe." She wrapped her arms around her ball of laundry and tried to think. Too much had happened in the last few days, and she couldn't understand it all. She tried to block out the confusion until she realized that Mama and Papa had come back to her for the first time since she had set foot in the Zedek house. Maybe they weren't gone after all!

Chapter Twenty-Nine

Sarah tugged at Luska's hand again. "We should go."

Jakob agreed. "You must be exhausted, Lala. Please, come home with us. You need to eat and get some rest."

She did feel tired.

As they started walking, Jakob pointed to her bundle. "Would you like me to carry that for you?"

"No thank you. I'd rather keep it with me."

"What do you have in there?"

My whole life, she thought as she held it tighter. "Everything I have left from my shtetl. Is the place where you're staying far from here?"

"Nearly an hour's walk. I will carry you if you like."

She was thinking about saying yes to his offer when a carriage turned the corner and parked in front of a house down the street. Jakob approached the driver as the uniformed man helped an elderly couple out of the cab.

Jakob motioned to Sarah and Luska to join him. "Let us ride back to the house." He lifted Luska into the carriage and then helped his wife get in before giving the driver instructions. "After he takes you ladies to the apartment, I shall continue to the town square to wire Mr. Smetana about our arrival." He climbed into the carriage.

"You were going to do that this morning, when we found Lala," exclaimed Sarah. "With all the excitement, I completely forgot about that."

"It is fortunate we asked Mr. Smetana for a second bedroom when we presumed your mother would move in with us. Now we shall give that room to Lala."

Sarah smiled, but it quickly faded.

The driver snapped the reins and the carriage lurched forward. Luska sat between the Hafsteins. The cab rocked gently as the horses drew it across the cobblestones, tipping Luska side to side between the couple. The movement lulled her. To keep from nodding off, she stared out the window and reflected on how different the city appeared now. It wasn't scary like at night, but it wasn't very pretty either, with gray buildings along gray streets against gray skies. Nothing like her village.

She sighed. "Where are we?"

"Near the old part of the city."

The elegant mansions with lush gardens had gradually changed to less grand houses on smaller plots.

"Where are we going?" Luska asked.

"Mr. Hafstein and I are staying at my mother's apartment."

"How far is it from here?"

"Not much further, a few more blocks past the next corner. It's nothing like the Rabbi's home, though."

"It's not big and fancy like theirs?"

Sarah chuckled. "No, it's very small and plain."

"Does it have a toilette?"

"Down the hall."

The carriage turned onto a narrow lane with modest homes cramped together on compact lots. She peered out at children playing in the street. Between the clip clop of the horses she could hear snatches of giggles and shouts. A woman in an old dress sang a wordless song as she hung laundry on a clothes line, while two men next door argued over how best to fix the broken wheel on their cart. It reminded her of home, of Mama and Papa.

"When are you going back to your country, Mr. Hafstein?"

"We leave tomorrow night on the train."

"How far away is it?"

"We will have to sleep two nights on the train to get there."

"What's it like there?"

"I do not know yet. We used to live in a very big city called Prague, but when we return, we will be moving to a new house sixty kilometers north of the city."

"Why? Is it because of the Cossacks?"

"No, fortunately. Do you remember the drop leaf desk I made for my sister? The one you liked so much?"

Luska nodded.

"I am a furniture maker by trade. Six months ago, a man came to my shop and introduced himself as the owner of a furniture company, with a factory north of the city. He told me he planned to expand the factory, which might put me out of business, and what a shame that would be since my work is some of the best he had ever seen, so would I consider working for him? After some talks, I was chosen to be the new head cabinetmaker."

"Don't be so modest, Jakob." Sarah prodded. "It's a big promotion for you, working for one of the best and most respected furniture companies in all of Europe, and a wonderful opportunity for us. No one knows us there, so we can make a fresh start. You too, Lala."

"That's what the Rabbi said about sending me away. What does that mean, a fresh start?"

"It means that we want to go someplace where people will get to know us for who we are, not what we were. The best way for us to do that is to move away and leave everything behind but each other."

"A fresh start," Luska repeated. "Everyone seems to want it..."

"*Each dawn brings a promise new.*"

"*...move forward and don't look back.*"

"...but I don't understand why. I would give anything to return to my shtetl and have my life back the way it was."

"That's because you've lost so much you think that no matter what you gain, it will never be enough. And despite the sadness, it's much easier to remember what you had in the past than to guess what you might have in the future."

Mrs. Hafstein not only spoke truthfully, but she also had a way of saying things so Luska could understand not just the words, but what they really meant. Not even Mama could do that.

She turned to Sarah and caught her sharing a secret look with her husband. They did that a lot. Her smile was wide enough to show teeth, her eyes would brighten and her face perked up. He grinned in a quieter way, but his upper lip would twitch a little and make his mustache wiggle. His eyes sparkled like they were lanterns, their light shining happiness. It reminded her of how Papa and Mama were at night, when they sat together in the kitchen while Mama did her mending. She could see the Hafsteins loved each other, like Papa and Mama did. She never felt that way about the Zedeks, though. They were pleasant and kind to each other, but they treated each other more like company than family.

"...we can make a fresh start. You too, Lala."

What she wanted, to go back, could never be. She would have to move forward. Not her heart, though. She didn't have to take that with her.

She could leave it behind.

Chapter Thirty

"Oy, I won't miss walking up all those steps!" Sarah grunted.

The carriage pulled up to a large, boxy looking house. Sarah and Luska got out so Jakob could continue to the town square.

They climbed up a steep flight of stairs, twice as high as the ones leading to the Zedek home, just to reach the front door. Once inside, they huffed and puffed up four more stairways that zigzagged to the top floor. The morning clouds had finally burned away and sunlight spilled down the top flight of steps that led to the roof.

Sarah pulled a key from her pocket and unlocked one of the two big doors in the vestibule. It opened into a dark foyer, but across from it was a sunny parlor. A narrow hallway that ran the length of the apartment connected all the rooms. Sarah walked ahead, past the parlor to a tiny kitchen with a plankwood table. As Luska followed, she admired the elegant pieces of furniture that seemed out of place in their humble setting. Though not as fancy as those she'd dusted in the Zedek home, they were as beautiful. The woodwork on a foyer table caught her eye.

"Did Mr. Hafstein make this?"

"He did. Except for a few older pieces that my mother acquired over the years, they're all his work. Come into the kitchen, dear, but be careful – there are boxes everywhere."

Stacks of crates and trunks filled most of the room. Luska sat at the table as Sarah filled a pot with water.

"Are you hungry, or would you rather take a nap first?"

"I'm not hungry or tired right now."

"Would you like me to show you to the room where you will be staying, so you can put your things away?" Sarah left the pot on the cold stove.

Luska followed her down the hall past the parlor to a small room facing away from the street. It held a small bed covered with a faded quilt, a nightstand, a chest of drawers and a hard-backed chair, and not much else. Little else would have fit in the small room, but the afternoon sun flooded it with golden light, so it felt warm and pleasant.

"Let me freshen it up for you." Sarah shook out the bedspread and fluffed the pillows. "This bedroom hasn't been used for a while…it was my mother's, may she rest in peace." She opened an empty dresser drawer. "You can put your things away here, if you like. I promise you, they will be safe."

Luska nodded, but held on to her bundle.

"Mrs. Hafstein, can I ask you something?"

"Of course."

"Why did the Rebbetzin tell me to make David's bedroom perfect for a little girl?"

"I suspect she wants to give that room to Esther now."

"But Esther already has a room, next to her parents."

"And that will be used for the new baby."

The Rebbetzin was having a baby? Maybe that's why she didn't want to keep Luska anymore. But Mama was having a baby, too, and she still wanted Luska.

Sarah sat on the bed. "You're awfully quiet all of a sudden. Is it because of the room?"

"Oh no," Luska assured her. "It's very nice." She went to the window. It overlooked a back yard, covered in weeds and wild grass, bordered by a rickety fence. In the yard next door, a horse with protruding ribs flicked its tail at flies, while scrawny chickens pecked at the dirt. Neat rows of potato and onion tops, beets, peas, and beanpoles sprang up from a small garden in the yard across the way.

"That looks so much like my shtetl," she sighed. "Especially that vegetable garden. Mama had a garden like that. She'd grow lots of potatoes and cabbage, because they were Papa's favorite. Mama used to make the best potato and onion soup. Sometimes we would eat it every day for a week. I never minded because it tasted so good, but Papa would always say, 'Mama, please, less onions and more potatoes'...." She turned to see if Sarah was still in the room and found her listening with a faint smile. Luska bit her lip and murmured, "I'm sorry. Maybe I'm not supposed to talk about them."

"Why would you think that?"

Luska thought back to all the times she tried to talk about Mama and Papa. "Because the Rebbetzin never let me. She would always say something to make me stop. She wanted me to forget them."

"She thought if you didn't think about them, it would hurt less, but we both know that doesn't work."

"I tried to, but I couldn't."

"You shouldn't have to. You can talk about them to me any time you want; Mr. Hafstein, too." She stood up. "I'm going to fix myself a cup of coffee. Can I get you anything to eat or drink?"

"No, thank you."

"You're welcome to stay here, or keep me company in the kitchen."

"I'll go with you."

Luska rethought her decision not to eat when she noticed the plate of cookies Sarah put out to accompany her coffee. She bit into a crisp ball of cinnamon scented dough studded with nuts.

"Mmmm, this is delicious."

Sarah nodded in appreciation. "My mother's recipe. They're not as good as hers, but they're close." She helped herself to another cookie. "My mother was a marvelous cook and a very talented baker. Go ahead, dear, have another."

197

Luska needed no further encouragement. She finished the cookie in two bites and eyed the last one on the plate before Sarah snatched it away.

"Don't ever take the last one, or you'll end up an old maid. My mother taught me that. I know it's an old wives tale, but why take a chance?" She popped the cookie into her mouth.

"But you just ate it!"

"Yes," Sarah smiled, "because I'm already married."

Luska giggled. "Why would being married keep you from ending up an old maid?"

"An old maid is a woman who never marries. You want to get married someday, don't you?"

Luska shrugged. "My Papa used to say 'A girl as spirited as my little Lala would catch the eye of a rich merchant's son,' but Mama would tell him, 'Since when have you ever shown any talent for predicting the future?'"

Sarah patted her hand. "No one can say for sure, dear, but knowing you, I'd wager on your Papa." She went to the icebox, poured some cream into a glass, mixed it with a little water and gave it to Luska.

"Try this. My mother always served this to me when I was your age."

"You miss her very much, don't you?"

Sarah's smile thinned. "More than I care to admit."

"Is that why you want to get a fresh start in the new town?"

Sarah sat back down at the table. "No, I'm sad that she's gone, but it wasn't anything like your situation. She lived a long life and died peacefully."

She swallowed the rest of her coffee. "Do you remember asking me why the Rebbetzin wasn't happy when Mr. Hafstein married me?"

Luska nodded.

"The Hafsteins were well-to-do, what the French call

198

bourgeois, and my family wasn't. She was so furious with us she convinced her father to disinherit Jakob, which is how the Zedeks can afford that modern house and all those expensive furnishings on a Rabbi's stipend.

"But the reason why Naomi did that is she didn't think I was good enough for her brother, and as you saw today, she still doesn't. That's why Mr. Hafstein and I don't want people to know about my past. You see, my mother was a servant."

"But you told the Rebbetzin there was nothing wrong with being a servant."

"Not with the work. It's an honorable profession, but if you're a servant, you're considered a second-class citizen. People don't want you to be anything but what you were born into. I don't think that's right. You shouldn't inherit your place in life, high or low—you should earn it."

She gathered the rest of the dishes from the table. "My parents were hard-working people. My father worked in the factory, and my mother was a housewife until he was killed in an accident. The poor woman had two children to feed and clothe, me and my little sister Hannah, who died a few years later, God rest her soul, so my mother had no choice but to enter into service."

She brought Luska's glass to the washbasin. "Fortunately, with her cooking and baking skills, she managed to secure some very good positions. Even so, she could prepare a wedding cake for her employer's daughter but not attend as a guest. And that station in life extended to her children."

"That's why you didn't want me to go into service for the Rebbetzin."

Sarah washed the dishes. "I felt you deserved better than that, and eventually, so did she. Every child should have a home, loving parents, a chance to go to school, to learn to read and write."

"But Mr. Vostok can read. I saw him reading a book."

199

"That's because he didn't enter into service until he was fourteen, when his father died. Anya, on the other hand, was born to servants. She began her training when she was about your age. She never learned to read or write, or play games—things a child should do."

"You mean like Saul and Esther?"

"They might not be the best examples, but yes."

Luska nodded.

"So do you still think going into service would have been a good idea, Lala?"

"No, but now I don't know what I'm supposed to do, what you said about having a purpose in life. What is my purpose?"

"That's something you will have to figure out as you get older." Sarah dried the dishes and stacked them next to the washbasin. "Anya tells me you have quite a knack for arranging things. You must be very artistic. Maybe you will be an artist when you grow up."

"An artist?"

"Someone who draws, or paints pictures."

"Like the one of the Rebbetzin?"

"Exactly. Artists capture what they see in life and put it on paper, or carve it in stone. In fact you could say Mr. Hafstein is an artist because he creates such fine furniture."

The idea of making beautiful things excited her. "Do you think I could ever make anything as nice as that patchwork chest, or the painting of the Rebbetzin?"

"Lala, I believe you can do anything you set your mind to—"

A knock at the door interrupted Sarah.

Chapter Thirty-One

"Rabbi?" Sarah said as she opened the door. "Is everything alright? Please come in."

Luska hid in the kitchen. What was he doing here?

She peeked from the doorway. Rabbi Zedek carried Esther in one arm, the other was draped around Saul's shoulder. Did he come to take her? Did she even want to go back?

The Rabbi nodded a greeting to Sarah.

"Please, call me Hershel. After all, we are family." He put Esther down. "How are you, Mrs. Hafstein?"

"Sarah."

"Sarah it is, or I should say Aunt Sarah. Children, this is your Aunt. Say hello."

"Good afternoon," Saul recited while Esther hid behind her father's leg.

"I came to thank you for bringing Lala back safely. We were terribly worried about her."

"Thankfully, she's fine. Please, why don't we go into the parlor?"

Luska peered down the dark hallway to watch. Sarah escorted the Zedeks to the floral-print sofa and took the low side chair for herself. Rabbi Zedek set Esther on his lap. Saul placed the small satchel he carried at his feet and sat next to his father.

"Vostok and I looked for her all night, but despite my prayers, we could not find her. I am so thankful you did."

"Perhaps it was your prayers that put Jakob and me in the right place."

"How kind of you to say that." He cleared his throat. "I

feel I owe you and Jakob an apology as well, for that, um, misunderstanding with my wife. You are fine people; I never doubted you would be good parents. I expect Naomi believes that, too, but sorrow can blind us."

"There's no need to apologize. These things happen in families. I can't even begin to imagine what she went through...." Sarah fell silent.

Esther was swinging her legs. The Rabbi stilled them when she kicked his shin.

"I brought the children to see Lala before she leaves with you."

Sarah stood up. "She's in the kitchen. Let me bring her in."

Luska fidgeted in the doorway. "I don't want to see them," she whispered.

Sarah took her hand. "That would be rude. They came all the way here to say goodbye."

She stood firm.

Sarah wrapped her hand around Luska's wrist and gave it a tug. "Come on, bold girl."

She followed Sarah into the sitting room. Esther beamed one of her sunshine smiles when she saw Luska, but Saul kept his head down. Luska wasn't sure if he was unhappy about coming to see her or embarrassed by what his mother had said. She suddenly felt very sorry for him, for as horrible as it was to lose Mama, losing your mother's love had to be awful, too.

"Hello." She meant it to sound cheerful but it came out in a near-whisper.

"It is good to see you, Lala," said the Rabbi. "Especially here, with your new family. I am so happy you will be living with such a wonderful couple. Are you happy as well?"

Luska bit her lip and said nothing.

He pulled his collar away from his neck. "The children brought you some going-away presents."

Saul handed his father the satchel. The Rabbi opened it and unrolled a dress. "This is from Anya."

It was the dress she had seen, half finished, in Anya's room, made out of her own curtains. Anya's kindness warmed her heart, but other memories of that day, of the darkness she felt wandering through the servants' quarters, rushed back to sweep away her good thoughts. Luska held the dress up against her. "It's pretty." She showed it to Sarah. "Miss Anya made the dress I'm wearing, too."

"What a thoughtful woman she is," acknowledged Sarah. "And talented with the needle."

Luska folded the dress with care. "Please tell Miss Anya I said thank you, Rabbi."

"I will. The children have a gift for you as well."

The Rabbi helped Esther off his lap. She took Saul's hand as he reached into the bag and pulled out a flat item wrapped in paper.

"Here," he said, handing it to Luska. "This is for you."

She removed the wrapping. Inside was the book about the Ash Girl.

"Esther, this is your favorite book. Are you sure you want to give it to me?"

Esther pointed to her. "You Ash Girl."

"But you said I wasn't the Ash Girl anymore."

Saul pointed to the back cover. "I read the book, too. Her life is frightful at the beginning, but in the end, she moves away and is happy. A good way to end a story, is it not?"

Luska flashed back to that morning when Saul ran upstairs after hearing his mother say those unloving things. She couldn't forget the sorrow in his face. Luska impulsively gave him a big hug. He allowed it. Before she let go, she whispered in his ear, "I know you like me. I like you, too."

He shrugged it off, but a little smile slipped out.

Sarah stood up. "Can I offer you something to eat? I don't have much, but I baked some cookies."

The children's faces lit up at the mention of sweets. Their eyes pleaded with their father.

"I think my children would enjoy that. Would you take them into another room, though? I wish to speak with Lala privately, if I may."

Sarah took Saul and Esther to the kitchen. The Rabbi sat on the sofa and gazed at Luska with sadness. Her stomach began to boil and she looked down, focusing on the gifts on her lap.

He leaned forward. "When I asked you earlier if you were happy now that you have a real family, you did not answer. May I ask why?"

"I don't know how I feel, except mixed up."

"I thought you wanted a home and a family, like you had before."

"No, I mean, maybe I did, but now...I, I don't know." Her temper rose with her frustration. "Everything's changed again. Now I'm in another strange house with people I hardly know, and they're going to take me far away, and it doesn't matter what I want or what I say...."

"The Hafsteins are wonderful people."

She took a deep breath. "They seem very nice, but they're strangers."

"You did not know us until the night you came to our house, but within days you felt as if you were part of the family. I promise it will be the same with the Hafsteins."

She thought of the Rebbetzin. "Sometimes people don't keep their promises."

"But I always have. I promised you I would find a good family to take you in, and I kept that promise."

Luska nodded. "But they're leaving tomorrow, and everyone says I have to go with them because," she waved her presents before him. "Because the Rebbetzin gave me to them like I was a gift!"

"Not a gift. An answer to their prayers. Mr. and Mrs. Hafstein were already very fond of you before today. When they came to see me and found out the little girl they had met at my house needed a home, the first question they asked was, 'What about us?' They have waited many years to be blessed with a child, and I assure you they will love you like a daughter."

There was that word again. Love. All love had ever done was cause trouble and pain. Mama and Papa loved her, and she loved them, but they were gone. She had thought she loved the Rebbetzin, but the woman had only pretended to love her. Why did everything have to be about love?

"Rabbi, if the Hafsteins want to love me, does that mean I have to love them back?"

He flinched. "Why, do you doubt you could love them?"

"I don't know if I want to."

"Why not?"

"Because every time I love somebody something bad happens. Loving hurts too much."

He patted the sofa and Luska sat next to him.

"Do you think closing yourself to love will protect you from feeling pain? No, child, closing your heart can only lead to pain. Caring about people and knowing they care about you is what brings joy into your life."

"But the Rebbetzin—"

"She was wrong." He took a deep breath. "My wife thought keeping her heart closed would protect her from suffering like she did when David died. But it has not, and now she also sees how much this has wounded her children, especially Saul. I tried to tell her that, but she would not listen to me." His head dropped. "I have always considered that my biggest failure, as a Rabbi and a husband."

He turned back to face her. "You finally made her understand that today, when she saw you making the same mistake. You taught her an important lesson—no matter how much it may hurt when you love, when you cannot love, it always hurts more."

She thought of the Rebbetzin mourning over the picture of David and wondered if anything could be worse than the suffering she saw in the woman's eyes.

"I'm scared, Rabbi. Too many things are happening."

He slipped his arm around her shoulder and gave her a gentle hug. "You have been through so much in the last week and it has left you adrift, like a petal in the wind. You are still mourning the loss of your home and family—really two families—and you feel overwhelmed by the thought of becoming part of yet another one. Then there is the biggest change. You will have to learn how to be a child again, free of the grown-up responsibilities you had to take on in your shtetl, and that may be the scariest thing of all."

As his words sunk in, tears of relief brimmed in her eyes. "I didn't…that's right…oh, Rabbi, you do understand."

He chuckled. "One of my 'chores' as a Rabbi is to understand and to help. Let me suggest something to make things a little easier for you. Try to think about one good change, something that would make you feel happy." He stroked his beard. "What about your new home?"

"All I know is that it's far away."

"In the countryside. Perhaps it will remind you of your shtetl in better days."

Her shtetl. Bad memories began and she shut her eyes to block them. But some good memories sprang up, too, like wildflowers in the meadow.

She shrugged. "Maybe."

"Have you thought about what it will look like? The color, the size? Will it have a yard with lots of trees?"

"Does it have a toilette?"

"Exactly, Lala. It is exciting, something to look forward to. Your future will be in that house. I want you to be able to enjoy it. Perhaps this will help." He reached into his satchel. "I have something else for you, from the Rebbetzin."

He placed the trio of figurines on the table. "She said, 'Use them to make your room perfect for a little girl.'"

"Does she want me to clean them for her?"

"No, child, they are yours to keep. Take them with you to your new home and when you look at them, think of us."

"Thank you." She didn't understand all this, which made her more confused and frustrated.

"...*like a petal in the wind.*"

Esther's giggling traveled down from the kitchen.

Luska was awed by how the little girl could enjoy herself anywhere. "I like Esther. She's always happy." Luska couldn't remember a time when she felt that carefree.

The Rabbi patted her hand. "You can be like that, too, Lala. All you have to do is open your heart."

Chapter Thirty-Two

The Zedeks said their goodbyes at the front door.

Sarah gave Hershel a small plate wrapped in a kitchen cloth. "Here are some cookies to take home with you. You can keep the dish."

He released Saul's hand and opened the satchel the boy carried. "That reminds me, I have one more gift in here, for you and Jakob."

"You didn't have to."

Hershel handed Sarah a black book. "It's a Bible, to record your new family history."

"How thoughtful. Thank you, Hershel."

"No, thank you again for everything you have given us."

"It was no bother. I baked plenty of cookies."

"I meant Lala, and especially Naomi."

Sarah waved her hands. "We just tried to help."

"Still, you managed to accomplish more in one afternoon than I have in two years. Coping with the loss was hard enough, but not being able to comfort her…"

"I wouldn't give up yet, Hershel. She may be a bit, um, emotional now, but she's a strong woman. My mother always said it takes more time to wear away rock than wash away sand."

He smiled. "My mother said that, too." He picked up Esther and swung her in the air, which set her giggling again. "We had best be going. You have much to do before you leave."

"We'll write as soon as we arrive in our new home." Sarah opened the door.

"Good. I promise our family will stay in touch." He

patted his son's shoulder. "Come, Saul."

Sarah closed the door behind them.

Luska went to the parlor window to escape the confusion she felt. Happy memories and dark thoughts rocked back and forth inside her head like a cradle.

Sarah followed her into the room. "So Lala, tell me what the Rabbi wanted to talk with you about, although you should probably call him 'Uncle Hershel' now."

The question stung her. "Why?"

"Because he's married to Jakob's sister, which would make him your uncle."

"No, why do you want to know what we talked about? Did he tell you what I said?"

"He didn't tell me anything...what did you say?"

"I don't have to tell you," she snapped.

Sarah's foot began to tap. "Young lady, I think we should have a talk about that temper of yours. Have a seat."

Fuming in silence, Luska plopped down on the sofa, her arms and legs crossed like a shield of flesh to protect her from Mrs. Hafstein's prying.

Sarah didn't say anything at first. She took a deep breath and let it out in a slow, loud whoosh. "Do you dislike being told what to do by anyone, or just me?"

"What do you mean?"

"I expect you did what your Mama and Papa told you to do."

Luska shook her head. "They didn't need to. I always did what had to be done without being asked. They only told me what they didn't want me to do. But then I'd say 'I can do it, let me do it,' and they'd always let me do it."

"You would say that and they'd agree?"

Luska thought about it. "I usually had to ask a lot, sometimes for many, many days. But I wanted to help them, and they, they..."

"They what, dear?"

210

"They needed me to do it. That's what I would say to make them change their minds, except about doing the laundry. They kept saying no, but then Mama told him, 'Papa, we have to let her go.'"

Her eyes filled with tears as the memory returned and the meaning of those words sunk in. "Everything's different now, but I don't know if I can be different, or want to be."

Sarah went to the sofa and threw her arms around Luska. It made Luska uncomfortable and she moved away. The Rabbi told her she should open her heart, but he didn't say she had to. Ignoring the pained expression on Mrs. Hafstein's face was another matter.

Sarah dabbed her eyes with a handkerchief and stood up. "Mr. Hafstein will be home soon. I should start dinner. Why don't you take a nap before we eat?"

"I'm not tired."

"Then why don't you lie down in your room and have some quiet time to yourself." Sarah tried to smile with little success. "I'll call you when dinner's ready."

Luska started for her room. Before she opened the door, Mrs. Hafstein called out, "You know, things might not be as different as you think. There's something my husband and I will need you to do, if we are to be a real family."

She stopped in the hallway. "What's that?"

Mrs. Hafstein's voice quivered, "Try to love us."

Chapter Thirty-Three

Luska sat on the bed and frowned. Her life was like rocks tumbling from a cliff, spinning and flipping all the time.

"Try to love us."

If Mama and Papa were here, what would they tell her to do?

The long shadows outside drew her to the window. She stared down at the vegetable garden that reminded her of home, of Mama.

Mama. She'd know the answer, if only she'd come back.

Luska turned away from the window. Her gifts from the Zedeks lay on the bed, ready to be stowed inside her bundle. As she loosened it, she noticed David's clothing tucked in there. They should be given back, she thought. As she pulled them out, the bodice of Mama's dress popped out, too.

"Since when have you ever shown any talent for predicting the future?"

Luska slumped on the edge of the bed, her thoughts muddled with whispers from the past. She took apart her ball of laundry until she found her Sabbath tablecloth rolled up in its center. She placed it in her lap and opened it to reveal the Bohemian crystal goblet. Its golden bowl sparkled in the late afternoon light.

Sounds from the past echoed in her head. She draped Mama's dress over the chair, then returned to the bed and tried to imagine Mama wearing it, sitting there in front of her. She stared and stared and stared....

A sweet, familiar voice called to her....

"How will I tell Mama about this?" Papa wondered aloud.

213

She curled up in Papa's lap. After listening to him repeat the story many times, it didn't sound as scary. She touched the goblet.

"Can I hold it, Papa?"

"Alright, but be careful. If it falls it will break." He handed it to her.

It felt heavy for its size. Her little fingers wrapped around the clear stem and base. The yellow bowl sparkled in the lamplight, like sunshine in summer.

"It's pretty, Papa."

He kissed the top of her head. "You deserve pretty things, more than your poor Papa can give you. But someday...."

"Someday what?"

Mama sat in the chair, next to the stove. Papa handed her the golden thread and the goblet. She held the goblet up to the light as he explained how the soldier used his saber to force the trade. Mama shuddered when he drew his thumbnail across his throat.

"Stop!" she cried.

He lowered his head. "I'm sorry to disappoint you, Mama."

"I'm not disappointed." She unrolled the thread to gauge its length. "Luska, bring me the Sabbath tablecloth."

Luska ran to the trunk where it was stored and brought it to her.

Mama spread it across her lap. She pointed to the center where her mother had embroidered a challah long ago.

"I finally know what I will add to this. I'm going to embroider a pair of Sabbath candles, one on each side, and use this gold thread to make the flames." She rolled it back into a ball.

Luska remembered this as clearly as if it had happened yesterday.

"Mama, can you hear me?"

Mama smiled at her. "Someday, when you are older, you will have to choose something to add to this cloth. I hope you won't have as much trouble as I did deciding what that shall be."

"I already know what I want to add." She held up the goblet. "This."

"That's a wonderful idea." She turned to Papa. *"We must keep it somewhere safe for Luska, for when she's older. It will be her treasure."*

"My treasure?"

"Yes, just like this tablecloth is my treasure. Someday, you will leave us and start a new family, as Papa and I did. When you do, you will take this tablecloth and the goblet with you. The tablecloth will be your heritage, because it holds your family history, but the goblet will become your treasure, for it will lead you to your new life."

"My new life? With who? How will I know where I should go?"

"You'll know, Luska. It may be something he says, or does, that means something special to you, but you'll know."

She took Papa's hand. "Trust your heart, for that is where we will be. Trust your heart."

The air began to shimmer and brighten as the ball of precious thread grew larger and larger, until the entire room filled with a blinding light. Then all went dark. When Luska opened her eyes again, she was slumped on the floor. The sun was gone and the shadowy colors of dusk filled the sky. She jumped up and looked around. Her tablecloth and goblet lay in the chair atop Mama's dress, but there was no sign of Mama or Papa. She picked up the goblet and nearly dropped it when she heard a knock.

"Hello Lala," Jakob called through the door. "May I come in?"

She laid the goblet on the bed and went to open the door.

"Did you get any rest?" he asked as he entered.

Luska nodded.

"Are you hungry?"

Good smells from the kitchen followed him into the room, but she just shrugged.

"Dinner is almost ready. Will you join us?"

"May I put some of these things away first?"

She took the tablecloth from the chair and laid it on the bed to reroll.

"What is that?" he asked.

"Mama's Sabbath tablecloth." She opened it up so he could see how it was decorated with generations of embroidery.

"My, what a treasure you have there."

"This isn't my treasure, it's Mama's." She picked up the crystal goblet and held it out for him to see. "This is my treasure. Isn't it beautiful? It comes all the way from Bohemia."

Jakob lingered in the doorway.

"Lala, do you remember the place where we are going to live?"

"Yes, near Prague."

"Do you know where that is?"

"Not really, just that it's far away."

He smiled. "Prague is the capital city of Bohemia."

Bohemia!

"It may be something he says, or does, that means something special to you, but you'll know...."

"Trust your heart...."

Papa kissed the top of her head. "You deserve pretty things, more than your poor Papa can give you. But someday...."

"Enjoy your life, child, and remember what I told you... move forward and don't look back...."

"Trust your heart..."

"Go."

She followed Jakob into the sitting room. Sarah put her sewing down as she entered. When Luska looked closer, she saw the tiny cross-stitches on the circle of fabric sealed in a ring. Embroidery.

"Trust your heart…"

She took a deep breath for courage. "I have something to tell you."

Chapter Thirty-Four

They celebrated over a simple dinner. Luska helped Sarah clear the dishes from the table and put them away after washing while Jakob made a list of all the boxes, crates and furniture they would take with them to Bohemia. Afterwards, they relaxed in the parlor.

Jakob rubbed his belly. "Wonderful meal, Sarah. Did you enjoy it, Lala?"

"It was delicious. Mrs. Hafstein, you're a good cook, just like Mama."

"Thank you, dear." She turned to her husband with a pained look.

Luska's stomach began to churn.

Jakob tented his fingers. "Lala, we need to talk to you about some very important things before we leave the country." He opened his desk and removed some papers. "First of all, you need to understand there will be some things about our past that must remain private – kept secret from anybody we meet in our new home."

"Like about Mrs. Hafstein's mother?"

"Only the fact that she had to go into service. All people need to know is that her widowed mother passed away recently, nothing else. This way we are telling the truth."

Sarah snorted. "Frankly, it's nobody's business."

"True, but these are the realities of life. There are other things as well."

"Like what?" asked Luska.

Jakob took a deep breath and exhaled. "We also want to tell everyone that you are our real daughter. But that would mean you must keep your past a secret as well. You cannot tell anybody about what happened to you before today...ever."

"But why?"

Jakob looked at Sarah, but she shook her head. "Maybe we can explain it to you when you are older, but for now, let us just say you will be safer this way," he said.

"Safer from what?" Luska wondered why he didn't want to tell her the real reason. Mama and Papa tried to hide bad things from her, too. It made her nervous.

"We didn't say anything before because we didn't want to frighten you," Sarah admitted. "We want to make sure you're safe from Cossacks. They know your Papa invented the latch. We're concerned that they may find out you survived. We don't want to take that chance. So can it be our secret?"

She never thought about the danger she faced. This last week taught her that she didn't understand things the way adults did. "Do I have to forget about my Mama and Papa?"

"No, dear," reassured Sarah "Not forget, but stow them away, in your heart, like you stowed your precious things in that bundle. Can you do that?"

"Trust your heart, for that's where we will be...."

She nodded.

"Good." He still looked worried. "Sarah, where is the Bible Hershel brought us?"

"On the table next to you."

He opened it to the front page, which had a scrawl of black ink on the bottom line and nothing else.

"Hershel signed it, but left the information part for us to fill out." Sarah fetched a pen for him.

He beckoned Luska over. "We are going to create our new family history in this Bible. Since it will become yours someday, I want you to understand everything I write in here." He pointed to the first line on the page. "Name – Lala Hafstein. Agreed?"

She nodded. He wrote it down.

"Next, date of birth – when were you born?"

"In midsummer."

220

"That could be August, or late July. Do you know the day, or the year?"

"No."

"How old are you?"

"I'm almost eight."

Jakob sat up. "Really? I would never have guessed, you look so much younger."

"Jakob, she can't be eight," Sarah claimed.

"But I am."

"We're only married seven years. You can't be eight."

"Sarah is right." He put the pen down as he mulled this over. "We will have to change your birthday. We were married in October, eighteen ninety-one, which means you would have to have been born no earlier than…late spring of ninety-two."

"What about today?" Luska suggested.

He thought about it. "That could work, and it is the first day of your life as our daughter. I like that idea."

"No, Jakob. It's too soon, and besides, we can't cheat her out of a birthday. Let's make it July twelfth, my mother's birthday; that way I won't forget." She smiled. "We can celebrate in our new home with a cake and presents." She repeated out loud, "Birth date July twelve, eighteen ninety-two. It will be a little close, but at least it should keep tongues from wagging."

"Settled. The rest will be easy. Parents – Jakob Hafstein and Sarah Hessen Hafstein, married October sixth, eighteen ninety-one. We are done. "

"Jakob, there's one more thing."

Luska yawned. "I'm tired, Mrs. Hafstein. Can I go to bed now?"

Jakob tapped his pen on the desk. "I see what you mean. Lala, no one will believe you are our daughter if you call us Mr. and Mrs. Hafstein. Pick whatever names you are comfortable with, as long as they are suitable for parents."

"I hadn't thought about that." What did children call their parents? Bella Vichenko called her father "sir." She looked at Jakob and shook her head.

"Goodnight, Mama. Goodnight Papa."

She shook her head again.

"Saul, I don't want to take your mother or your father away from you...."

Mother and Father. They seemed happy when she said it aloud.

Jakob clapped his hands. "Alright, daughter, it is time for you to go to bed. We have a big day tomorrow, much to do before we leave."

They walked her to the bedroom, where her possessions were still sprawled across the bed. Sarah found a small satchel which she gave to Luska.

"Take this to carry your things on the train. It will be much safer and easier than trying to manage that bundle."

She can be so kind, Luska thought, always doing simple things to make me feel at ease. Luska saw the admiration in Sarah's eye as she folded her tablecloth. Maybe someday she would ask her new mother to embroider something on it, too. Someday. Maybe.

She packed her clothes, the goblet and the tablecloth, and then studied the remaining shtetl laundry spread across the bed. "What shall I do with all this, put it in the poor box?"

Sarah folded Mama's dress and Papa's good shirt. "I have a better idea."

Chapter Thirty-Five

They stood before an open grave in the forest. Jakob had paid a cemetery worker to dig it a meter wide and half a meter deep, and place two big rocks at the head. A shovel, left behind to complete the burial, jutted out of a mound of dirt. Luska gripped her bag as Sarah unfolded Mama's dress.

"On which side of the bed did your Mama sleep, dear?"

Luska pointed to the right.

Sarah laid the dress along the right side of the grave. Jakob put Papa's shirt to its left. Together, they recited the prayer for the dead, and then, one by one, laid a pebble on each of the stone grave markers.

"I want to talk to Mama and Papa alone, please."

Sarah began to say something, but Jakob gave her hand a gentle tug. "We shall wait in the coach until you are ready."

When they walked away, Luska stood before the grave.

"Mama, Papa, I leave tonight on a train that will take me to Bohemia. It's very far away. I hope you can find me there, but maybe you won't be able to, so I want to tell you something before I go.

"Remember how unhappy you were when I would beg you to let me do chores? I understand why now. You wanted me to do things that children do, like play with dolls and go to school, not fetch water and do laundry. But you needed me to do it, so you'd always give in.

"I know you felt badly about it, but don't. I wanted to help, and not because I was in a hurry to grow up, Papa. I thought having nothing to do meant you had nothing. So that's why I wanted to do everything – because I thought I had everything. I had you and Mama, and nothing else mattered.

"And Mama, I also know why you always worried about money and having enough for us. I'll have plenty of food and clothing now, and I'm going to start school, so you don't have to worry about that anymore. But I've learned that even if you're rich, money can't make your pain and sadness go away. A wise Rabbi told me to open my heart to love. Maybe he's right. I always felt safe and happy with you and Papa, even in winter, when we huddled around the stove with nothing to eat but stale bread."

She caught her breath as fresh tears streamed down her cheeks.

"I love you both so much and I miss you every day, but I have to go on, like you told me in my vision. Mr. and Mrs. Hafstein will take care of me now. They're nice people, you'd like them. I don't love them like I love you, though. I don't know if I ever can, or even want to. But I'll remember what you said. Maybe someday I'll make a new place in my heart for them, next to where I keep you."

She blew a kiss into the grave. "Goodbye."

Jakob and Sarah returned to finish the burial. He filled the shovel with dirt and extended it to Luska.

"Take some and toss a little bit over each side."

She scooped up a handful and watched it trickle down on Papa's shirt, then on Mama's dress. Jakob readied the shovel over the mound of dirt.

"Wait," she cried. She removed her two shtetl dresses from her bag. The one she wore on the day of the pogrom, made from Papa's shirt, she placed in his side of the grave, wrapping his shirtsleeves around the bodice in a hug. She laid the other dress, the one she dirtied while scrubbing the Zedek's house, on top of Mama's dress.

Luska watched in silence as the clothing gradually disappeared under the dark soil. With it went all the joy and

224

love she had ever known. But she found comfort in knowing that, even though she couldn't have Mama and Papa, she would at least have the life they wanted for her.

A hand gently stroked her hair.

"Your Mama and Papa finally have the burial they deserve. Do you want to keep the rest of the laundry from your shtetl?"

She shook her head.

"Is there anything else you want to do before we leave for Bohemia, Lala? Lala?"

Lala. Everyone knew her as Lala now. From here on, Lala she would be. The girl once known as Luska, and all the heartbreak she endured, would remain here, buried in an unmarked grave under the Russian forest.

Chapter Thirty-Six

Lala curled into a ball next to the third window in the train car. It was where the porter escorted her when she and the Hafsteins first boarded the train to Prague, and where she wanted to stay ever since that evening. The turn of events at the gravesite left her dazed and feeling out of place. Unfamiliar sights and foreign voices added to her sense of disconnection. Rather than saunter through the cars to explore the train, she spent much of the time staring out her window, lost in thought, wondering what lay ahead. She kept thinking about what the Rabbi had told her. What Mama had said. Outside, as farms and villages, meadows and forests rushed by, she captured all those images in her mind. Perhaps someday she might try to draw them.

She noticed the Hafsteins seemed concerned by her quietness and lack of curiosity at first, but they did not intrude beyond an occasional stroke of the hair or pat on the cheek. She found their low-key manner calming, their warmth reassuring. By the last evening she sat between them, which they seemed to welcome, for their faces radiated silent pleasure. She held fast to her bag though, never allowing it to leave her sight.

"How far away is the town where we're going to live?"

"At least a four hour ride from the train station. We should be there before dark." Jakob told her.

"When do we get to Prague?"

"Not for several hours. Are you hungry?"

She smiled. "A little."

"Then we shall all have a treat."

Jakob escorted them to the dining car.

"Let's order three different pastries," Sarah suggested.

"Then we can all try each of them."

"By that, do you mean you will try to eat all three pastries?" He winked at Lala. "Better hide your candy from your Mother, Lala. She has a real sweet tooth."

"You're poking fun at me." Sarah pretended to be annoyed. She gave him a playful jab in the belly. "Now I'm poking some fun at you."

Lala giggled. She enjoyed the way they teased each other, for their affection was obvious.

The waiter took their order. "Would you care for something to drink, sir?"

Jakob waved his finger between his wife and himself. "Coffee, with cream, and our daughter will have...what would you like to drink, Lala?"

A girl from the shtetl would ask for tea, she thought.

"A glass of milk, please."

They reached Prague shortly after lunch. Lala kept close to Sarah and Jakob as they maneuvered through the stifling passageways. A few steps ahead strode two porters who were transferring their luggage to a coach that would take them to their new town.

The station felt hot. It smelled of sweat, stewed meat, and cabbage. The noise and bustle reminded her of the evening she first arrived in the city. A man selling flowers caught her attention. She turned her head for a moment to admire the pretty blossoms and quickly thought better of it.

When she turned back, she couldn't see the Hafsteins. Panicked, she froze in place as people milled past her as though she wasn't there. Her eyes scanned the crowd...where were they? Images of wandering through her destroyed village, fleeing in the forest, running through the streets of the city flooded her mind.

No, no, no…she could not bear this again, all alone…

A group of men a few meters in front of her moved aside to walk across the tracks. That's when she saw her parents, waiting patiently for her. She ran to them and as she approached, they each extended a hand. Lala seized them firmly. Her father took her satchel and carried it for her as the three of them continued to the exit, where a coach awaited that would bring them to their new home.

Lala held fast to her parents' hands and didn't let go for a long, long time.

Coming in 2015 – A Petal In The Wind Book II – Lala Hafstein

Miko Johnston first contemplated a writing career as a poet at age six. That notion ended four years later when she found no "help wanted" ads for poets in the Sunday New York Times classified section, but her desire to write persisted. After graduating from New York University, she headed west to pursue a career as a television and print journalist before deciding she preferred, to paraphrase Mark Twain, the more believable realm of fiction. Her short story, "By Anonymous," was published in the Sisters In Crime anthology *Last Exit To Murder.* Miko lives with her rocket scientist husband Allan on Whidbey Island in Washington.